Married
by Lunchtime

... A Short Story ...

Peter Gatenby

Contents

Chapter 1

Be careful what you wish for.

Alfred sat on the patio just outside the French-doors that led into the conservatory. He was wearing his tweed jacket and britches and had his legs crossed displaying his smart walking shoes. He finished reading his paper, leant back in his chair and said to Amanda in a slightly exasperated tone,

"Well, are we going on this walk then?"

"Oh, Alfred, you know I don't like to be hurried on Saturday mornings."

She continued to slowly eat her grapefruit, and, although she was only dressed in a pink bathrobe, did not give any sign of concern for Alfred or give any intimation that she might hurry off to get dressed.

Some men might have felt slightly awkward sitting next to a slim blonde so scantily dressed, even perhaps secretly excited wondering if she had anything on underneath.

Suddenly, Amanda said, "I wish something exciting would happen. I'm bored; maybe we should invite some new people to the party tonight?"

"Who, for instance?" asked Alfred.

"Anybody," said Amanda.

"I don't think that would be a good idea at the moment."

"Why?" queried Amanda in a slightly annoyed voice.

"Because there's some chap going around attending house parties in Buckinghamshire and stealing jewellery."

"Really? How do you know?" asked Amanda in a slightly excited voice.

"It's in the Telegraph."

"Oh, let's see; show me!"

Rather reluctantly, Alfred handed Amanda the paper and after a few moments, she started to read aloud: 'Police have so far been unable to pin the thefts on anyone although they admit they are following certain lines of enquiry and feel confident of an arrest soon. A police spokesman said, "We are dealing with a young opportunist who was probably athletic and agile'.

Amanda continued as if daydreaming; "Probably tall and dark and went to Eton or Harrow..."

"And will be knocking on your door asking to attend tonight's do," said Alfred in a disapproving tone.

But Amanda wasn't listening. She was excited by the vision of this swarthy 'Raffles'-like person who would slide into her bedroom late at night, make mad love to her and then slip out with her pearls.

"My pearls," she said out loud, as the full aspect of her thoughts hit her. "No, not my pearls; that awful brooch that Aunt Grace left me. It's quite valuable but ugly; I won't miss that."

"There's a gentleman to see you, Miss Amanda."

Amanda swung round, shaken out of her daydreaming. She looked up to see Harman, the butler. She realised that Alfred had given up and gone off on his own, or to seek out Diana, his long-term girlfriend.

"A gentleman?" said Amanda slightly confused.

"Yes, Miss, tall, dark and carrying a small briefcase. Says his name is Mr Julian Radiant. Shall I show him into the drawing room?"

"No, send him out here," said Amanda impatiently.

"Shall I say you'll see him once you've had time to dress?" Harman was always a stickler for correctness.

"No, no, send him out here now."

"Eh... Umm, very good, Miss."

Amanda's heart was racing a little. Was this the man the police were looking for? She was half afraid yet excited. She untied her long blonde hair so that it swayed in the slight breeze. She quickly tidied the table placing the breakfast items on a tray, then sat down, crossed her legs and waited.

"Miss Amanda Charlecote will see you in the garden, Sir, if you would follow me."

A tall stranger stepped from the conservatory into the warm sunlight closely followed by Harman. "Mr Julian Radiant," announced Harman.

Amanda looked up but said nothing, just held out her hand. It was uncanny; he was just as she had imagined only a few minutes ago. About six foot, dark, slim build, yet clearly athletic. He stood to attention, bowed slightly and took her hand with a warm but bold grasp.

"Very pleased to meet you, Miss Charlecote."

Amanda managed to get her voice back and, as Harman turned to leave, said, "Could we have some fresh coffee, Harman, please?"

Harman paused, looked slightly put out and then said, "Very well, Miss."

"Poor Harman," said Amanda once he was out of earshot. "He does like things to go to plan and you arriving has upset his schedule."

"Oh, I did not mean to be a nuisance," said Julian. "Perhaps I should leave."

"No, no, I want to find out how you do it... I mean, who are you?... I mean, well, is your name real?"

"Well, just about," said the stranger in a jovial voice. "You see, my grandfather came over from France, and got fed up with the English not knowing when to pronounce a 'g' as hard or soft like *marga-rine* or *margarine*, so, he changed it from Ragiant to Radiant, except he failed even then as I am often called *Radi-ant*."

3

"How intriguing," said Amanda. "I would never have guessed your name, but you are just the right height, and your hair is dark as I imagined."

Amanda trotted this out without really thinking; she was already under the spell of this handsome stranger. Julian, however, was somewhat taken aback, then, composing himself slightly, he noticed that the paper was open at the article headed '*Church gains from gate-crashing jewel thief*'. "Oh, crumbs, she must already realise who I am," he muttered under his breath.

"Oh, I do; you see, I'm born under Capricorn; we have the instinctive ability of knowing what is right and we are also telepathic," said Amanda.

"When were you born?"

"Eh, 7th May," said Julian obediently.

"Oh, Gemini," said Amanda. "At least you have a sense of humour."

He laughed and looked down at her long hair. Suddenly, realising how little she had on, he felt somewhat vulnerable. He felt he should leave; matters were not going to plan. Normally, he did the talking; he took control, yet it had taken this young lady only a few moments to discover his identity and she probably knew the original motive for his visit; for all he knew, the next thing she would do was call the police.

As Amanda poured the coffee, Harman reappeared. This time, he stood bolt upright and said in a deliberate tone,

"There's an Inspector Rathbone from Aylesbury CID wishing to see you, Miss Amanda. I showed him into the library."

Clearly shaken by these words, Julian looked about to see whether he should make a run for it, but Amanda suddenly took control of the whole situation passing Julian a cup of coffee and forcing him to sit back in his seat.

"Julian," she said in an over-affectionate tone, "you should have rung to let me know you were coming. If I had not received the letter from your aunt saying you were a great one for just turning up, I might have wondered who you were. Now, you must stay for lunch. Harman, another one for lunch and tell that Inspector fellow to come out here; I don't know what he wants but I suppose we had better be polite to him."

She turned to Julian and said, "Don't worry". Then she let out a squeal of excitement – "Ooh! At last, something exciting!"

Julian, however, felt slightly sick but said nothing.

"Inspector Rathbone," announced Harman.

"Oh, do come through, Inspector."

"Good morning, Miss Charlecote." He eyed the dark stranger and continued, "I wonder if I might have a word with you, *alone*, Miss."

"Oh," said Amanda seeing the Inspector's nose twitching as he examined poor Julian. "This is my cousin, Julian Radiant; you can say anything you want in front of him."

"Well, er..." said the Inspector, who was clearly trying to decide whether to accept this cousin story or make an arrest and check things out later, but with Amanda's shapely form beside him, he turned to Julian.

"Do you live locally, Mr Radiant?"

By this time, Julian was feeling like a man who had not only been caught naked but with the jewels around his neck.

"No, London," said Julian, but seeing the Inspector was not impressed, he continued; "Richmond, actually, on the hill near the park." He dared not give his actual address so chose that of a work colleague. Then, plucking up a little courage, he asked, "Do you know it?"

"No," said the Inspector. "I lived for a time north of the Thames at Ilford, but I have never been to Richmond."

"Not born under Capricorn then," said Julian, half under his breath.

"Capricorn, sir?" enquired the Inspector.

"No, I'm Capricorn," interjected Amanda, "and Julian's Gemini. What's your birth sign, Inspector?"

"Eh, Libra," said the Inspector who felt slightly put out as he should be the one asking the questions.

Julian laughed; "I suppose it would be - justice and all that."

The Inspector said nothing; he was getting nowhere.

"Can I offer you some coffee or perhaps something stronger?" Amanda suggested with an air of devilment.

"Er, no thanks, Miss. I've come on a serious matter if I might have your attention." He laboured the last word trying to take control, but it was no use as Amanda continued her questioning.

"Someone stole one of your police cars?"

"No, I mean really serious."

"A bicycle, then," said Julian cheekily, eyeing Amanda.

"Mr Radiant, if you must know I am investigating a series of robberies from large houses similar to this one. The suspect is a young man who would fit your description precisely. I understand there is some kind of a 'do' here tonight and hey presto, who has just arrived, but you, Sir. Now, can I have some straight answers? Otherwise, I shall be forced to ask you to come with me to the station."

The Inspector was clearly annoyed and looked straight at Julian.

"Where were you last Wednesday?"

Julian suddenly felt undressed again.

"Er, St Albans," he said. Although this was a lie, it was the first thing that came into his head.

"And what were you doing in St Albans?"

"I went to buy a book."

"Any particular book, Sir?"

"A set of books actually by Wordsworth." Julian had suddenly remembered that he had once been to St Albans to sell such a set of books a few years back when he was briefly a rep for a publishing company, therefore, he thought he could now provide such detail that the Inspector may not investigate too closely.

"And why go all that way to buy this Wordsworth feller?"

"Because I sold them a set a couple of years ago," Julian answered with a slight air of triumph since this bit of the story was true.

"And what did you do that evening? Why, St Albans can only be a couple of hours' drive from Buckinghamshire."

Suddenly, Julian paled. He thought he had been clever, but of course, he knew the burglaries took place late in the evening.

"He stayed with my aunt," said Amanda.

Julian looked up at Amanda with slight astonishment.

"That's how I knew Julian might come today because she wrote to me saying that Julian might call. What's more, if you want to know where I was, Inspector, I was...."

She was about to say the Walker's house, but the Inspector cut her short.

"No, Miss. I'm quite sure we are looking for a man..."

But Amanda was not really listening. The hairs on the back of her neck had risen when she realised, she had nearly destroyed the alibi she had created for Julian, for it was at the Walker's that the last burglary had occurred, and she could have been his accomplice!

The Inspector droned on, "...and, in order to be sure there are no further burglaries, I would be grateful if I could have one of my constables attend tonight's proceedings!"

Amanda was initially a bit annoyed by having some clodhopping constable getting in the way, but then she thought about the challenge of stealing right under the noses of the police and warmed to the idea.

"Well, okay," said Amanda.

"What time shall I send him round, Miss? He better be early," said the Inspector.

"Seven o'clock, I suppose," said Amanda.

"Well, I must be going," said the Inspector who took a long and detailed look at Julian and strode back through the conservatory. He was confident he knew who the culprit was, but decided that as he had little evidence, just a mere description, it would not be worth making an arrest *yet*, but he thought to himself, 'This evening... who knows?'

As soon as he had gone, Amanda leapt across and kissed Julian on the cheek. "This is going to be a great weekend; do you ride?"

"Er, yes," said Julian who was now completely shattered by the whole experience, "but I haven't any boots or gear."

"Oh, don't worry. We'll borrow Alfred's. I'm sure they'll fit you."

Chapter 2

Is this Real?

"Race you," said Amanda.

"Where to?"

"The church," said Amanda and sped off.

Julian took a little while to get the feel of his mount but was soon galloping behind. The church stood about a mile down the valley, but its bell tower could clearly be seen over the trees. After half a mile, Julian had caught up and they were jumping fences and hedges like a couple of professional steeplechase jockeys.

"Where did you learn to ride?" said Amanda, slightly out of breath.

"I worked in stables at Newbury for six months," said Julian, who then quickened his pace when he saw the gravestones of the churchyard up ahead. With a show of daring, he cleared a three-foot stone wall then a line of gravestones and pulled his mount up just below the church tower which conveniently struck the half-hour, as if to announce their arrival.

Amanda, now clearly beaten, trotted in through the open gate and dismounted, leading her horse round to where Julian was standing.

Julian led the horses across to an area of rough grass and secured them to some iron railings.

Then, taking Amanda's hand, he led her into the church. They walked a few paces into the church, side by side, then Julian stopped, put his arm around Amanda's waist, and bowed his head but said nothing. In truth, he was a little out of breath. He felt like a character in a film who, in a few short minutes on screen, would experience all the emotions of fear, suspense, exhilaration and love. He found himself momentarily transfixed as his eyes focused on the altar cross. "Is this real?" he asked himself. He looked round at Amanda who, in turn, looked into his eyes. He turned away thinking to himself, 'She really is beautiful; this can't be real.'

"Ah, I'm glad you're punctual," said a voice from behind.

An older man with long grey hair was walking towards them. He was dressed in a priest's attire.

"The Reverend Stanshawe has been called away to Wales as his mother is gravely ill. He asked me to fill in for him. I'm Sydenham Merver; strictly, I'm retired but I'm happy to help out. Delightful church, is it not? Dates from the 13th century you know, although rebuilt in 1856."

"Yes," said Amanda. "I was christened here."

"Excellent, excellent," said the priest. "It's so nice to have people married in the church they've grown up in. It makes it more of a family occasion; people feel more at ease. Come now, come now; stand here. Now, where's that prayer book of mine?" He felt about his robes and produced a large but well-worn prayer book.

"Dearly beloved, we are gathered here in the sight of God... Erm, we'll miss out that bit for now; let me see..."

"We're not here to get married," said Amanda.

"Oh, don't worry, this is only a rehearsal anyway. We don't have any witnesses so it would not be valid, so to speak. Now, I want you to open your prayer books at page 302. Oh, young man, please get two prayer books from the shelf back there. That's right, the red BCPs."

"But we..." stuttered Amanda but she was cut short by the insistent priest.

"Doesn't matter, doesn't matter. God won't worry about the jodhpurs, even on the day, as long as you love him and he loves you, that's the main thing."

"But the banns haven't been read," said Amanda.

"Oh, we'll soon sort that out."

Julian returned and handed Amanda a prayer book. "Let's pretend," he said in a whisper.

"Oh, okay," said Amanda looking at him and giggling.

"Never thought I'd be married by lunchtime," whispered Julian.

"I told Harman to put the champers on ice," chuckled Amanda.

The priest went through the main points of the service, explaining each part and getting them to rehearse their vows. It was the first time they had really looked at each other. They both felt like they had been chosen to act in a play, and this was a technical run-through.

Julian half expected someone to shout 'cut' or 'can't hear you', but, this time, nothing happened. The priest finished going through the service, noted down their full names and where they had been baptised then shook their hands warmly and said, "I'll leave you two lovers together," and disappeared as quickly as he had arrived.

Amanda squeezed Julian's hand gently then they turned and walked slowly out. Neither was smiling; it was as if both had realised that this might not be a dream.

As they rode back, Amanda started to ask questions. "Where do you really come from? Is it Richmond?"

"No," said Julian. "I was brought up in a church orphanage in Clerkenwell."

"That explains it," said Amanda in a matter-of-fact way, as if to convince herself that deep down, he was really an honest man. "You only did it for them. You're like a modern-day Robin Hood."

"And what do you do?" said Julian, trying to change the subject. "And where are your parents?"

"Oh, they died nearly two years ago in a car accident."

"So, you live all alone then!"

"Well, in theory, although I have a younger brother at university and my uncle is always around. I think he feels it's his duty to look after me. He's only about 14 years older than I am but he's so boring."

"Is that Alfred then?" asked Julian.

"Yes. How did you guess?"

"I'm wearing his boots!"

"Oh, of course!"

Keeping the horses at walking pace, they continued to fill each other in on their immediate past like a couple of long-lost cousins. Then arriving back at Cooper's Bank, as the sign on the gate indicated, rubbed the horses down, led them to the stables, and, having put up a couple of nosebags, strolled in ready for lunch.

Chapter 3

The Challenge.

Lunch was served in the dining room, but with only four of them, they might have done better in the kitchen. Julian again felt like he had been placed in a film set. Harman was forever bobbing about serving this or that. Julian did not eat a lot; he still couldn't quite grasp what was going on. Previously, he had merely obtained an invitation to the 'do' and remained as ordinary as possible so that later, no one would be able to precisely identify him. He did this by speaking in a multitude of accents and styles of delivery. He had learnt this technique from his fellow orphans who came from many backgrounds, but Amanda knew more about him than anybody, except perhaps a few close friends at work in the city or former bunk mates at the orphanage.

With Amanda and Julian sitting opposite each other, the foursome was completed by Alfred and Diana. Diana was a lady-in-waiting and waiting she had been for about ten years; waiting for Alfred to ask her to marry him. However, it had never quite come to that. It had been sort of understood that when Alfred felt he had established himself as an outstanding barrister, they would marry. He had a couple of minor victories under his belt but awaited the 'great case' that would bring him forward into the public eye.

After lunch, Julian and Amanda went walking in Ramscoat Wood, chatting about this and that till they finally sat down under a large beech tree.

"What are your plans for tonight?" asked Amanda.

"That's very much up to you," Julian replied.

"I mean, will you steal the jewellery during the party, or later, at about 2 am?" said Amanda, looking for clarity.

"Er, well... Am I invited to this party then?"

"Of course, you are you're the star attraction. I mean to me, that is." As she said this, Amanda shuffled her shoulders in a slightly coy fashion and then leant across and stole a kiss.

Julian paused for a moment and then, taking her cheeks in the palms of his hands, gently kissed her on the lips. Amanda put her arms around his neck and pulled him towards her. When Julian was finally released from this embrace, he took a deep breath and said softly, "I shall not steal anything."

"What?!" exclaimed Amanda "You've got to! I mean, it won't be fair if you don't."

"You mean you actually want me to steal some jewellery from you?" asked Julian in bewilderment.

"Yes!"

"Why?"

"Because... because it's exciting, romantic; only, you mustn't steal my pearls. Promise me, whatever else you steal, you won't steal my pearls. They were a present from my mother on my 18th birthday and her mother, my grandma, had given them to her on her 21st birthday."

"Okay, I promise," said Julian laughing, "but I will steal one other thing."

"What?"

"A kiss," and taking hold of Amanda, he rolled her over on the grass and kissed her on the lips and neck until, giggling, she cried out, "Enough! No more; you mustn't, not here anyway."

Julian was not expecting this; did she really mean what she had just said? This conquest was becoming too easy.

Amanda continued, "First, you must steal something without me knowing and then bring it to me on the stroke of midnight."

"And where will you be?" asked Julian.

"I'm not going to tell you, but if you find me before the hall clock stops chiming twelve, then I will... I will give you the key to my heart," she said rather dramatically.

Julian repeated the challenge slowly to ensure he had it right.

"I steal something, but not your pearls, presumably a piece of jewellery and then I have to bring it to you as a sort of token."

"Yes," said Amanda, "but if you don't find me by the stroke of twelve, I shall cry 'thief' and Inspector Rathbone will whisk you away in his Black Maria!"

"You have a wicked sense of humour."

"Well, do you accept the challenge?"

"Okay," said Julian. "Now, do I deserve another kiss? I may not get another one!"

"Just one," said Amanda and puckered her lips.

Julian leant forward, but, after a fleeting moment, Amanda pushed him away and stood up.

"Come on, we must get back and see if Adrian and his crew have arrived."

"Who's Adrian?"

"My brother; He's bringing a load of his friends back from university and knowing Adrian, he will be bringing competition for me, so you'll have to watch out someone else doesn't whisk me away when you're not looking."

With that, Amanda strolled off leaving Julian sitting on the ground trying to decide whether she was just playing with him until a more desirable man turned up, or whether their relationship was deeper than that.

When they had stood in the church, he had felt a sense of belonging to each other. Yet now, she was willing to gamble him away. He had found it hard to decide his own feelings towards her, for just when he was willing to steal for her, she had now made this remark about being some sort of trophy for her brother's cronies and this had upset him.

While Julian remained seated on the ground, Amanda had now disappeared out of sight. Julian looked around; several hedge sparrows chased each other round a hawthorn bush. As he leant against the beech tree, a robin cheekily landed on a bough which bent down and almost touched the ground. He leant back and closed his eyes trying to make sense of the day's events.

Chapter 4

The Chase.

As Julian relaxed against the tree, he was just about to doze off when he heard the sound of a horn; then, coming closer, the sounds of dogs barking. The noise began to grow louder, and he realised it was a pack of hounds. Surely, they would not come charging through here? He looked back in the direction of the sound, and, feeling threatened, decided he better get back to the house. He rose to his feet and had hardly gone two paces when he tripped and fell sprawling into the leaves. A large red-brown furry animal barked in his face and then sped off, disappearing into a bank not twenty yards away.

As he stood up a second time, he brushed the leaves out of his hair and noticed a strange smell; "Fox!" he said to himself, and, in the same breath, "The hounds!"

This time, he just ran, quickly realising that he was the quarry. "How fast can hounds run?" he wondered. "Well, I suppose they have to follow on horseback... *Ye Gods*!" and he ran faster.

He tore along the path but realising that he had to find some way of slowing his pursuers, took a less well-worn track. It soon narrowed and he found himself fighting to avoid birch twigs from hitting his face. He also had to jump over brambles. As he raced on, he took little notice of where he was heading. The path started to descend and just as he thought it was starting to clear, it became even steeper so he half-ran, half-stumbled down the bank. Fighting to maintain his balance, he reached the bottom and was faced with a stream. His momentum was such that he could not stop but just had to make a brave leap to clear

17

it and reach the far bank. Alas, landing with one foot in the water, he slumped in a heap on the far muddy bank. As he scrambled upwards away from the stream, his hands, face, and clothes became covered in mud. Reaching the top, he was confronted with a close-meshed fence with barbed wire across the top. There was no time to find a way round so, taking off his jacket, he folded it in two, laid it across the top of the fence and hurled himself over.

The hounds could hardly be heard and were obviously slowed by the obstacles that had severely tested his own agility.

In a defiant mood, with the house in sight but at a distance away, he marched towards it. He soon came to the formal gardens around the house and climbing up a series of steps, he heard voices. Looking up at a first-floor window, he saw that a crowd had gathered.

"Amanda, what did you do to the poor chap?" said one voice.

"Hey, Julian, what happened to you, man?"

"I got chased by the hounds," said Julian, still slightly out of breath.

"Hounds chase foxes, old boy, don't you know!"

"Yes, but I fell over the fox."

"You what?"

"As I started to come back, I tripped over the fox. I smell terrible and as far as the hounds were concerned, I was the fox."

"What happened to the fox?"

"Oh, he was alright; he went to ground not twenty yards from where I bumped into him."

"Incredible!" said another voice. "Anyway, come around to the back door; you look awful."

"Okay," said Julian, now feeling a little dejected and stupid and as he wandered round the house, he heard shrieks of laughter which he assumed were at his expense.

He arrived at a rear door which opened as he approached. He was greeted by a young man with fair hair and dark eyes like Amanda's -

Adrian, he thought.

"I'm Adrian; Amanda's been telling me all about you. You are definitely flavour of the month, old chap. Pah, perhaps not smell of the month though! If you take those shoes off and follow me..."

Julian followed Adrian up some rear stairs till they arrived on the first floor outside a bathroom.

"If you would like to scrub down, old boy, I'll find something for you to wear. You look about my size and build."

"Thanks," said Julian who was cheered by the sight of this appealing oasis.

He shut the door, ran a bath, and having shed his muddy clothes, sank slowly into the steaming pool. As he leant back to relax, his instinctive reflexes took over and he found himself sitting bolt upright looking around the bathroom half expecting something, or somebody, to leap out at him. He then felt rather silly again as the large wave he had caused slurped over the edge of the bath wetting the carpet. Reassured, he calmed himself and relaxed again only to be surprised by a knock on the door.

"I've put some clothes outside the door, Julian, and some sneakers of mine that should fit. What size are you?" said Adrian.

"Nine," said Julian.

"Great," said Adrian. "See you downstairs in the lounge when you are ready; no hurry, but I've got a little surprise for you."

This last remark had Julian worrying again, but he decided to seek temporary solace in his warm, watery cavern and, leaning back, began to relax at last.

It must have been at least half an hour later when Julian woke with a start. He had fallen asleep in the bath and the water was now becoming cold, so he quickly finished his ablutions, checking every vestige of mud was gone from his hair and his face. Stepping out of the bath, he dried himself and then remembered the clothes outside the door. He tip-toed over, opened the door slightly and peeped out. There was nobody about, but below him was a neat pile of clothes and a pair of brown shoes, so he scooped them up and retreated back into the bathroom.

Adrian had thought of everything. Julian dressed slowly then stood up to examine the result in the mirror. The outfit was well thought out; brown sneakers, brown trousers, cotton floral shirt over which had been provided with a white polo-neck fisherman's jumper.

"Not bad; this Adrian has taste," he said to himself. Then, seeing his mud-stained clothes, he realised why the laundry bag had also been provided. He placed the filled bag, minus a few personal items, by the door. He then made sure the bath was clean of mud and the bathroom was generally tidy before starting on his quest to find Adrian and party. He decided to take the passageway leading away from the stairs he had come up, as he felt he would have a better chance of finding the lounge.

As he walked towards the sound of distant voices, Harman the butler appeared.

"Excuse me," said Julian, slightly sheepishly, "I've left a bag of dirty clothes in the bathroom back there. Any chance of them being cleaned?"

"Leave it to me, Sir; Mr Adrian warned me you may be needing assistance. They are awaiting your company in the lounge, Sir; if you take the main stairs just around the corner, the lounge is downstairs on the left."

"Oh, thank you," said Julian. "That's really kind of you."

Julian continued until he reached the stairs and was about to descend when he paused. "Oh, what's this surprise Adrian mentioned? A duel with the Master of the Hunt for spoiling the chase perhaps?! Oh, stop it," he reprimanded himself. "I'm getting paranoid. It's probably quite harmless." Then, taking a deep breath, he stepped boldly down the stairs. Near the bottom, he missed his footing and stumbled, fighting to regain his balance. "Delayed shock," he convinced himself and took another deep breath.

Chapter 5

Bat and Trap.

"Julian, is that you? In here."

Julian sheepishly entered the lounge and spotted Amanda with a group of girls in a corner. When they saw him, the little group huddled closer together and exchanged glances. This was followed by squeals of delight as Amanda continued her story. 'Obviously about me,' thought Julian.

"Hi! Come and sit here," said a voice. "I'm Charles and this is Harry, Alfred you met at lunch I believe, and this is Fleet", he said, pointing to a bronzed tall man with straight black hair. "He's half Blackfoot Indian."

"I was christened Christopher," said a deep voice, "but my grandfather still calls me *Fleet of Foot* as I'm a good runner. We seem to have something in common with you outrunning the hounds!" and he held out a hand which Julian accepted.

"And this," said Adrian, "is for you. You've earned it; in fact, qualified for it would be a better description."

There before him was placed a full half-pint pewter tankard.

"It's okay," said Charles. "It's just mulled wine, but I think you're in need of sustenance, old chap."

Julian reluctantly took the tankard and sipped it - it was quite strong and fruity, but he could not deny he was in need of a drink - 'Before something else happens,' he thought. Then he began to relax as he realised that this was a genuine present without any trickery or strings attached.

"How come I'm the chosen one?" asked Julian.

"Well," said Adrian, "it has become a tradition that we play Hares and Hounds on Sunday morning after a party. The Hares have about a 200-yard start which is taken as the stile as you enter the woods. Everybody then races off to the pub via Willett's Monument, which is on the far side of the wood, and the church, where at least one each of the two parties must enter a name in the visitor's book with time as well as date."

Charles continued the explanation; "Needless to say, our local pub is called the Hare and Hounds and that's how the idea arose. If the Hares get there first, the Hounds pay, but if they get caught, then they pay. Arrival is marked by the ringing of the bell that is normally rung for last orders."

Adrian continued; "As there are only four Hares, if they get caught then it can be bit expensive, since there are usually a dozen or more Hounds. If you think they should easily be first to arrive with a 200-yard start, bear in mind they are roped together round their waists."

"Well, sounds a fair challenge, as long as you are a reasonable runner," said Julian with a smile.

"Indeed," said Adrian, "but as you did it single-handedly, we felt it only right you should be rewarded," and the group burst into gales of laughter.

"Well, thanks very much," said Julian who was now warming to this slightly eccentric crew.

"Ever played 'Bat and Trap'?" asked Harry.

"No," said Julian, "that's a new one on me."

"Can you play cricket?"

"Oh, yes."

"Well, you'll have no trouble then. You need a good eye though; it's tip and run, but you'll soon pick it up; we usually have a game later if it's dry."

While Julian listened, he glanced towards Amanda who was still relating matters to her cronies, but presently, she stood up and wandered over to where the boys were sitting and sat on the arm of the chair beside Adrian.

"Have you told everybody what we've got in store for them tonight?" she asked Adrian, taking a sideways glance at Julian.

"Just filling them in, Mandy. What time's the food going to be ready? I'm starving; haven't had anything since breakfast, except for a couple of beers," he said laughing.

"And half a pork pie," said Harry.

"Yes, half a horrible pork pie served by a horrible barman in a pub just north of Newbury," went on Adrian.

"About half seven I thought," said Amanda, "and I think that's the rest of them arriving now."

There were the sounds of cars drawing up and doors being opened and shut and a general hubbub as people trooped into the house.

Julian wished Amanda had acknowledged him, perhaps sitting next to him rather than her brother. He felt jealous as a multitude of people came in and gave her a hug. Indeed, two of the guys gave her a kiss which she reciprocated. It wasn't that he wasn't accepted or made welcome, it was just that his thoughts had gone briefly back to the wedding rehearsal in church.

"And this is Julian," said Amanda.

Julian stood up, startled out of his misconception.

"Pleased to meet you," he said, holding out a hand and grinning, and feeling warm inside; Amanda hadn't forgotten him.

"I'm Jane," said a tall, slim, dark-haired girl.

"Em, you can steal my heart any day," she said, digging Amanda in the ribs.

"Sorry," said Amanda "he's promised to steal mine, when the time's right," Amanda said looking directly at Julian.

'So, the deal's on,' he thought, although he wished Amanda hadn't quite treated him like some knight-errant who had been charged with carrying out some deed that would lead to death or glory.

"Okay, everybody," said a voice from the back of the crowd. "The food is ready in the dining room and save your umbrellas; blue are one team and red the other; you'll see what I mean when you get there."

The melee moved slowly into the dining room. Julian soon realised his escapade with the fox was the main talking point, as snatches of conversation mentioning hounds or foxes could be heard from different corners of the room. He found himself standing with a group he had not met previously, balancing a paper plate of cold chicken and salad on one hand and eating with the other.

"What do you do?" asked a curly-haired bespectacled man of about 23.

"I'm a stockbroker," said Julian.

"Really? You mean in the city?"

"Yes," said Julian.

"Thought you must do something in the country with all these antics you've been up to."

Clearly, the story had been expanded, thought Julian.

"So, during the day, you dodge your way round bulls and bears and at weekends, you outrun foxes and hounds!" This remark caused a wave of laughter to echo round the group.

Julian decided there was no point in disclaiming the events of the afternoon so interjected with, "Yes" and occasionally, "I go on a stag hunt" and the group dissolved into laughter again.

After more banter and much nibbling, Adrian called the party to order.

"Okay, everybody! *Bat and Trap;* but there's so many of you to speed things up and add a little spice to your performances, every other person will be blindfolded."

"Blindfolded!" said several of the girls and a voice continued, "Can't hit the thing with my eyes open!"

Julian turned to see that the voice belonged to Jane. "Then you'll get your usual high score!" He smiled.

"Cheeky devil," she said. "Oh, blue, great! You're in my team," said Jane as she spotted the cocktail umbrella lying on Julian's plate.

"Come on, we are going to need athletic chaps like you," and taking Julian's arm, she led him through the hall and out into the grounds via the lounge.

Bat and Trap turned out to be a sort of cricket for small gardens, although, in this case, a full-size cricket pitch could have been placed on the lawn and even then, only occupy a small portion of the acres available. However, the reduced size did make everybody feel more involved. The wicket was just two slats of wood arranged so that if the ball hit one, the other fell down and you were out.

Alfred turned out to be an expert, scoring 6 before being caught out by an agile young girl in a blue mini skirt. Julian only managed to score two, but, as he was one of those blindfolded, he was satisfied with his score. In fact, he was a bit amazed; he had imagined Amanda sending him telepathic messages of when to swing his bat, and on this basis, had swung the rounders-type bat and, to his amazement, had connected with the ball. Someone had shouted 'cheat', but this was quickly forgotten as on the return run, he tripped over the trap and scraped his shin. Eventually, the reds one by six and Alfred claimed victory as if he had been the only one to score in his team.

As the party dissolved into little groups playing silly games or just chatting, Julian decided he'd better give some thought to his late-night quest. He suddenly realised that he did not actually know where Amanda's bedroom was, therefore, he walked aimlessly round the whole house looking up to see whether there was any clue, but while a couple of bedrooms to the rear of the house looked more palatial, there was nothing to confirm his suspicions. He would have to go inside and take his chances. He was becoming slightly unnerved by the whole thing.

Previously, it had been fairly simple - enter a likely room, go to the dressing table and open the drawers. He worked on the basis that valuable or sentimental items would either be clearly on view or locked away. The items that people were not so worried about tended to be at the bottom of jewellery boxes which were easily accessible. He could not be certain of this method of selection, but he only wanted to take pieces that would be reclaimable under insurance and not cause too much distress. He had found that pieces with sentimental value would be placed with valueless items such as flowers, cards, locks of hair or even love letters. These he had avoided. On one occasion, when he had been disturbed and had to depart in a hurry, he had picked up a small jewel-encrusted cross which, he discovered later on closer examination, had been inscribed on the reverse - *J I am with you always, V.* He had decided not to sell it via his usual fence, but to return it. However, rather than risk direct communication, he had sent it to the church orphanage with a type-written note saying where it should be returned. Somehow, the press had got hold of the story which accounted for the headline in this morning's Telegraph.

His other ill-gotten gains had been turned into cash first. He had trusted a person who he knew would part with cash for suitable pieces of jewellery. He had overheard a conversation in a pub and followed the man and made a note of the address. He then anonymously mailed the jewellery with instructions to send the cash to the church orphanage. He had to trust the man to do this for he did not want anybody to be able to identify him. This had worked perfectly well as the fence had a supply, if a little irregular, of easily disposable items and obviously felt it was a small task to satisfy this strange unknown benefactor by passing a commission on to a church orphanage.

Time was running out; it had gone eleven o'clock and on entering the house again he was accosted by various people who slowed his progress. Finally, he boldly mounted the stairs and walked purposefully along the corridor towards the larger rear bedrooms. This apparent audacious move he always felt was best and seemed to be effective. Sneak up some side-stairs and someone was bound to be coming down and question your purpose, but go boldly up the main flight and everybody assumed you had permission and knew where you were going.

He arrived in front of the two large rear bedrooms. "East or west?" he asked himself. Then he remembered Amanda had been dressed in only a bathrobe that morning and decided she was probably a late riser, so the sun in the morning would disturb her slumbers. "West it is then," he decided and quietly pushed the door open and slipped inside.

Chapter 6

An opportunist
and a thief.

Julian slid quietly into the bedroom but, rather than turn the lights on, went over to the dressing table which was in front of the window. Aided by the moonlight, he could tell that this was indeed Amanda's room and, as if by way of confirmation, a coloured silk scarf which she had worn that afternoon was tossed over one side of the mirror. He closed the curtains and turned on a small table lamp that rested on a tallboy at the side of the room.

He had a nagging feeling about this whole episode. He began to feel it was a trap - he felt silly stealing from somebody who knew he was going to do it, even though the prize, if you could call it that, was rather desirable.

He began to apply his usual method of selection. The necklaces, which had been tossed in a heap with several brooches lying on a small floral china tray, were clearly often worn, but of little value and were easily lost in the plethora of odd toiletries such as talc and perfume that bedecked the dressing table. He systematically opened drawers, starting with the column on the left side. They were all full of clothes, so he pulled out the middle drawer. Here were a few items of value - a silver bracelet, an odd ring - even a gentlemen's tie pin, but nothing that struck him as worth stealing. He continued down the right-hand column of drawers until the bottom one revealed several jewellery boxes. "This looks more promising," he said to himself. He was about to open a small red box when he heard voices outside in the corridor.

"Ah, Alfred, have you seen Julian?" said Amanda's voice.

"No, why do you want him? I was hoping you had gone off him; he spells trouble to me. A person who gate-crashes at 9 o'clock in the morning is not to be trusted."

With these words, Julian felt very vulnerable and quickly turned off the light and moved quietly round the dressing table crouching down between it and the window.

"He's my guest. I asked him to stay," said Amanda defensively.

"Well, he's an opportunist and a thief and you know it," said Alfred.

"How do you know that?"

"Because he fits the description of that fellow who stole from the Walkers the other week; we barristers have a feel for these things."

"Well, you'll have to prove it," said Amanda and stomped off.

"I shall," said Alfred and moved off into his own room next door.

Julian was a little shaken by this outburst - he was being brought back to earth with a bump. It seemed everybody must have known who he was, and yet only Alfred seemed to worry.

He looked at his watch and saw 11:48. "Crumbs, no time to lose". He returned to the dressing table and located the small red box again. He opened it and inside was a brooch with a silver clasp holding a large blue turquoise. Although moderately valuable, he did not care for it but thought it would do so, closing the box, he placed it in his trouser pocket. He was about to close the drawer when his attention was drawn to a black jewel case with a dog rose lying on top; it was the same rose he had given Amanda that afternoon.

He paused for a moment then realised this was a sign. He took the case out and tried to open it, but it was locked. 'Predictable,' he thought, 'but where's the key?' He looked about the dressing table, peered into odd pots then opened the middle drawer again, but nothing. "There's got to be some clue in here as to where she'll be," he said to himself.

He looked about the room. Close by hung a picture and he realised

it must be Amanda's mother. "That's it," he said. Peering behind the picture frame, he spotted a small key hanging on a concealed hook. Taking the key, he placed it into the lock, turned it and the box opened to reveal a note from Amanda lying on top of a double row of pearls. He read *'In the garden house, love Amanda'.*

He placed the rose inside and was about to close it when he noticed two locks of hair tucked in a pocket in the lid. There were two portions of golden hair, one with a small blue ribbon and one with red. 'I wonder whose,' he thought. Then, closing the box, he replaced it exactly where it had lain and, folding the note, he placed it under the box. He then closed the drawer and replaced the key.

The apprehension of the last few minutes had gone. He turned off the light and tip-toed to the door and opened it slightly; no one was in the corridor, so he quickly exited. He then nonchalantly strode towards the main stairs.

When he arrived at the top, he looked down to see people milling about but no one was taking particular notice of him, except possibly Alfred who seemed to eye him then brushed passed him and went up the stairs.

Although Julian had not been in the Garden House before, he knew where it was. He looked at the hall clock - six minutes to twelve.

Unbeknown to him, Amanda had seen him come down the stairs and needed to know whether he had found the note, so she doubled back through the dining room and kitchen and round to the back stairs which she climbed. Travelling down the corridor, she turned the corner and heard Alfred's door click shut. She quickly entered her own room and went over to the dressing table and opened the bottom right-hand drawer. The note was there but no pearls. He had taken the pearls after he'd promised not to! The swine - the barefaced cheek! All feelings of tenderness towards him disappeared. She was furious and rushed out of the room. Standing at the top of the stairs, she spotted Julian who had been temporarily waylaid by Jane.

"You thief!" she shouted at Julian. "You devil! You've stolen my pearls; how could you?"

Everybody stopped talking and looked up. As she rushed down the stairs to accost Julian, a hand beat her to it.

"Got you," Inspector Rathbone stepped forward. "I thought you'd slip up eventually; seems we have you red-handed this time."

Julian felt like a young puppy caught stealing the steak from the pantry. He did not protest - there was no point.

"Empty your pockets on the table," instructed the Inspector.

From his trouser pocket, Julian reluctantly pulled out the red box containing the brooch and placed it on the hall table.

"But it was agreed!" he protested. "I haven't got the pearls!"

The Inspector opened the box and looked at the brooch. "Is this yours, Miss?" he asked, turning to Amanda.

"Well, yes," said Amanda "but..."

Inspector Rathbone cut her off.

"That will do for starters. Probably hidden the pearls somewhere else so he can retrieve them later. Book him, Sergeant," and a plain clothes officer, who had unobtrusively been observing the proceedings since seven o'clock and was slightly annoyed at the Inspector turning up at precisely the right moment, led Julian out to a waiting police car.

Inspector Rathbone continued; "and tell Constable Simpkins to search for these pearls in Mr Radiant's car and anywhere else relevant. Now, Miss Charlecote, if we could go somewhere a bit quieter so I can get answers to a few questions," said the Inspector.

Amanda moved towards the library but was not really listening to the Inspector. She was looking at Julian who looked so pathetic being led away. He mouthed some words to Amanda - "I didn't steal the pearls" and shrugged his shoulders. At this, Amanda suddenly felt a pang of doubt. Had she wrongly accused him? But if it wasn't him, then who?

She opened the door to the library and began to answer the questions put by the Inspector, although she was not really concentrating.

"And I assume this brooch is yours?"

Amanda was shaken out of her ponderings. "Well, yes, but you can't arrest him for stealing that because I asked him to steal it."

"You what?!"

"I asked him to take it; it was agreed he could take anything but my pearls."

"Can you explain slowly, Miss, how Mr Radiant was asked to steal your jewellery? Is this some kind of joke? After all, wasting police time is a serious offence."

"Oh, I know, but I thought he'd stolen my pearls."

There was a knock on the door and Constable Simpkins peered in. "Excuse me, Sir, but I thought you would want to know we've found them; the pearls that is, in the gent's car, Sir."

"Right, now we're getting somewhere," said the Inspector with an air of satisfaction. "Get them down to the forensics lab and check them out for fingerprints. Where exactly were they found?"

"In the glove compartment," said Simpkins.

"Pretty obvious but that's his style; bare-faced effrontery," remarked the Inspector.

"Are you going to check the glove compartment for fingerprints?" demanded Amanda. "After all, he may not have put them there."

"Whose side are you on now? Anyway, you let us worry about that; okay, see to it, Simpkins."

"Okay, Sir," and Simpkins exited the library.

Meanwhile, Amanda was thinking back to when Julian had been led out. There had been something about the expression on his face – a mixture between bewilderment and annoyance. Not the sort of reaction from someone who was guilty. After all, Julian had been reluctant to steal anything, except... except a kiss, she thought, and a slight smile came over her face.

"Where exactly were the pearls kept, Miss Charlecote?"

"In a drawer in my dressing table."

"Show me," instructed Inspector Rathbone.

They left the library and turned into the hall. People were still hanging about slightly confused, not knowing whether to continue the party or not.

Inspector Rathbone told Simpkins to take a note of everybody's name and address and roughly where they had been between 11:30 pm and twelve. After that, they would be free to leave.

Amanda and the Inspector trailed upstairs to her bedroom. She moved over to dressing table. The bottom drawer was open.

"They were in there," she said.

The Inspector looked into the drawer. "Anything else taken or disturbed, Miss?"

"Only the note." Her voice faded as she wished she had not mentioned it and instead, had quickly picked it up and put it in her pocket.

"May I see the note, Miss?"

"Well, it's personal, you see, I......"

"Sorry, Miss, but this is getting a little tedious; if I could see the note."

Amanda reluctantly handed it over and the Inspector read it.

"Er, this seems to back up what you said earlier; you were obviously expecting him."

"Well, yes, it was agreed."

"I'm beginning to wonder whether there is a conspiracy going on here," said the Inspector.

"If it wasn't for the fact that this Mr Julian fits the description of the person we've been looking for in connection with previous similar thefts, I think I might quietly forget the whole thing. Now, are you or are you not accusing this Julian chap of being a thief?"

"Yes, we are," said a voice.

Alfred had entered the room and continued, "People like him need the full weight of the law brought against them. This man is clearly an interloper and a thief and, in due course, I shall prove it."

"Well, I'm glad somebody round here is sure of something; you are, Sir?"

"Alfred Charlecote. I'm Miss Amanda's uncle and guardian until she is 25."

"Well, thank you, Sir. Now I think I have all I need for the moment, so I'd better go and interview Mr Radiant down at the station."

Chapter 7

The hares won.

By the time Inspector Rathbone had arrived at the police station, Julian had been fingerprinted and was seated in the charge room guarded by a seasoned officer, Sergeant Wetherall.

Julian's mind wandered back through the events of the day. The bright early morning sunshine, the surprise alibi given by Amanda, the dream-like wedding rehearsal, the flight from the hounds and even turning this into a triumph as he became the talk of the party, but now he was totally defeated. He sat limp and depressed, feeling lost and very alone.

He did not feel particularly aggrieved, just mentally exhausted. He wanted to go back to yesterday - at least he had been in control. Now he felt like a man who had been exhilarated by a ride on a roller coaster only to be deposited into a pool of cold water at the bottom.

"Right," said the Inspector shaking Julian out of his daydream. "Could you tell me exactly what you have been doing this evening? I believe you had been playing some games."

"Bat and Trap," said Julian.

"And what happened after that?"

"Don't remember precisely; probably went and got a drink."

"And at what stage did you go upstairs to Miss Amanda's bedroom?"

"About 11:30 but it was purely a sort of game. It was agreed I would steal something; it was a sort of test to see if I could steal something right under her nose, so as to speak; and yours, come to think of it! I then had to take it to her by twelve o'clock. The difficult bit was she wouldn't say where she was going to be."

"So, shortly before Miss Amanda accused you of stealing, you were trying to find out from people where she was."

"No, I already knew by then."

"How?" asked the Inspector.

"She left a note."

"Ah, yes, the note; this one, I assume."

The Inspector pulled it out from his pocket and placed it on the table.

"What puzzles me," said the Inspector, "is why you came back into the house shortly before 12 o'clock; presumably the garden house is outside."

"I didn't! I was on the way there but got held up by Jane."

"Well, perhaps you went down the back stairs, round the house and in through the drawing room."

"No, I came down the main stairs."

"But you must have gone outside at some stage, Mr Radiant."

"Why?"

"To go to your car, remember?"

"I didn't go to my car."

"Well, we found the pearls in your car's glove compartment."

"I didn't put the pearls in my car, and I didn't take them. I agree I looked at them but that's all. I had to open the box to read the note."

"You mean the note was inside the jewellery case?"

"Yes."

"So, your fingerprints will be on the case?"

"Yes, but I didn't take them. I just put the rose back in the case where the note had been."

"What rose?"

"The dog rose that I had picked for her on our way back from riding this morning. Amanda had left it on top of the case as a sort of sign."

Julian's thoughts drifted back to their gentle ride home from church that morning and how he had picked the rose from a bush that was hanging over their path.

The Inspector pondered over this new evidence. It was such an unlikely story that he was tempted to believe it. Yet, the weight of evidence so clearly pointed to Julian that it was very difficult to see how anyone else had the time or opportunity to be acting in sympathy with Julian and not bump into him. Indeed, if someone else had stolen the pearls, they would only have had minutes to act if Mr Radiant was in the bedroom at about 11:45, and why choose Julian's car to hide them? No, this idea was ridiculous; he must be lying. Yet, when did he put the pearls in the car? It was such a small piece of the puzzle; if only he would just admit it, the case would be closed.

"Well, perhaps you'll change your story in the morning," said the Inspector. " In the meantime, you'll be charged and spend the rest of the night in the cell downstairs."

Julian nodded looking rather glum and was led off to be charged and locked up for the night.

Surprisingly, Julian slept through the night because he was exhausted both mentally and physically, and although his predicament had been worrying, it had not stopped him sleeping.

He awoke to the sun streaming in through a skylight. A clock on a wall opposite his cell told him it was just coming up to 7:30 am. He began to ponder how he could clear his name. He would get bail then get Amanda to clear the matter up. Somebody else had stolen the pearls and as soon as she realised it, the police could start looking for him. Strange, he thought, why the other person decided to act last night. It must have been somebody at the party who could have been at the Walker's, but why frame him by putting the loot in his car? It did not make sense. What did they hope to gain?

Eventually, at 8 o'clock and much to his surprise, Sergeant Wetherall

41

arrived not just with a cup of tea but with a full breakfast which his wife had produced.

"This is very kind of you," said Julian.

"Well, you're not the usual sort of villain we get in here; you seem too much of a gentleman," said the Sergeant. "Besides, it may be strange for a police sergeant to say this, but I think you may be innocent!"

"I am," said Julian "but someone must have decided to frame me, but besides trying to decide who, I can't understand why. After all, before yesterday, I didn't really know anybody although a few faces looked familiar."

"Well, perhaps I shouldn't be saying this, but Mr Alfred Charlecote seems to have it in for you. He was on the telephone last night wanting to know whether you had admitted to the theft and all the other recent burglaries. Apparently, he has been retained by the Walkers to sue you for the return of some property that went missing after a party a couple of weeks ago. I must admit I've never heard of such a situation before. Then Mr Alfred, being a barrister, seems to think in a different fashion to ordinary folk."

"I don't think he likes me," said Julian." I overheard him last night calling me '*a person not to be trusted*'. The trouble is I admit I was in Amanda's bedroom, but I definitely didn't steal the pearls. I admit I had a peep but, after reading the note, I put them back. There was no point. If I had wanted to steal them, I would have grabbed them and run. Somebody else must have put them in my car."

Did you have much to drink last night, Sir?"

"No not really. Surely, if you think I was blotto and didn't realise what I was doing, you would have noticed last night!"

"That's true, but drink affects people in strange ways and the shock of being caught could have sobered you up."

"No, I was only drinking the occasional half of bitter. I admit I did have a half-pint of mulled wine before we ate, but that was at about quarter past six, nearly six hours earlier."

"Well, if you think of anything else, let me know, but at the moment, all the evidence is firmly against you."

"I know, but I honestly didn't do it," said Julian, slightly annoyed.

"Well, enjoy your breakfast, Sir," said the Sergeant as he left the cell closing the door behind him.

Julian ate the breakfast slowly. He began to realise he was stuck there for the whole day and as the thought dawned upon him, he became rather depressed; he'd never been locked up before in quite this way. At the orphanage, although they'd be confined to their dormitory, it did not stop them slipping out of a window if the situation demanded, and, in any event, he had rarely been alone; but here, there were bars on the windows.

He daydreamed about how things might have been; a night of passion, breakfast seated at the foot of his goddess Amanda; Harman serving exotic fruits on gold dishes and the Inspector arriving on a chariot. At this point he giggled to himself and his eyes re-focused on the blank buttermilk wall in front of him. "Buttermilk," he said to himself and smiled again.

The hours passed slowly. Perhaps he should confess and get the matter over and done with, but no, why should he? He was innocent. He might be willing to admit to the other thefts, particularly at the Walkers, but no, not the pearls.

Eventually, the clock showed twelve and about twenty minutes later, he heard voices above. After a while, the door opened, and Sergeant Wetherall entered carrying a tray upon which stood a full pint tankard. "Mr Adrian has persuaded me that you are entitled to this, Sir. I am to make sure I say, the Hares won."

Julian beamed. "Well, at least I've still got some friends," he said quietly.

"Seems that way, Sir. They even tried to persuade me that it was all

43

a mistake, and that you ought to be released, but I'm afraid it's out of my hands. Now, if you don't mind drinking this up, Sir; if the Inspector catches me serving you beer, there'll be all hell to pay."

"Cheers," said Julian, suddenly feeling he might yet triumph and win the hand of the fair maiden. He made short shrift of the pint and returned the tankard to the tray.

"Please convey my thanks to the Hares," said Julian.

"Very well, Sir. I had better get this evidence back to the pub next door," and the Sergeant, acting more like a butler than a policeman, returned upstairs with the tray.

Chapter 8

For the sake of a rose.

At 2 o'clock, Inspector Rathbone walked into the police station.

"Any change in the patient?" he enquired sarcastically.

"No, Sir," said Sergeant Wetherall "He still maintains he's innocent; reckons he must have been framed."

"Well, if that's so, by whom?" questioned the Inspector a little frustrated. "I've been over and over the whole matter and if anyone else had stolen the pearls, they would have had to know our lad's every move to avoid bumping into him. The only people who could have done that are Amanda herself and Mr Alfred and what would be the point?"

"Well, Mr Alfred Charlecote seems dead against this fellow," remarked the Sergeant.

"That's true," said the Inspector, "but I think he just being overprotective. Besides, he's a barrister; I can't see a barrister going around fabricating evidence. What had he got to gain? Even if he's not keen on Amanda marrying Mr Radiant, she's over 21 so he couldn't stop her anyway. No, he must have done it even if he does not remember doing so. Anyway, besides last night's escapade, I've got Mr Walker coming around with his daughter to see whether she can identify him as the person who may have been involved in their burglary. If it is him, this will open up the whole case. He certainly fits the description. It also means he's less likely to get bail when he appears before the magistrate tomorrow."

"Does that mean you want an Identity Parade lined up?" asked Sergeant Wetherall, "only it may not be easy being Sunday afternoon. We need people of similar age and looks, or the exercise could be meaningless. Also, shouldn't we let him see a solicitor?"

"Has he requested one?" asked the Inspector.

"No, that does not seem to have crossed his mind."

"Well, better ask him if he wants one just to be on the safe side, but in the meantime, where can we get at least eight men similar to him?"

"There is one possibility, Sir, but I'm not sure you'll agree. You see, all the party crowd turned up here at lunchtime trying to persuade me to release him. They seemed to think he was a *good chap'* and they said the whole thing had been a mistake. I said it was out of my hands, but I got the feeling they were genuinely worried about him. Mr Adrian Charlecote seemed particularly concerned."

"Was Miss Charlecote here with them?" enquired the Inspector.

"No, Sir. I got the impression she had been persuaded not to come."

"Okay, that seems a good idea. Get them here for 4 pm. This could, in fact, be to our advantage as some of them may well have been at the Walkers' do, so if they pick him out, it will be a check that they really recognise him as the villain. If we got a load of farm labourers in here, it would not be much of a test; also, I think we had better let his solicitor know the situation."

"That could prove difficult, Sir. His solicitor if he has one, probably resides in London, notwithstanding today is Sunday."

"Well, see if we can find someone even if it's only temporary."

"I'll have a word with him, Sir."

Sergeant Wetherall took the keys, walked downstairs to the cell and unlocked the door.

"Oh, hello!" said Julian. "Is this a social visit or an official one?"

"Official, I'm afraid; there have been certain developments. Originally, when you were first charged, you said you did not want a solicitor, but I've been asked to ensure you understand the position. Only there could be further charges and it may be in your interests to take professional advice."

"What do you mean?" asked Julian, puzzled.

"We are arranging an identity parade for 4 pm for someone who reckons you may be the person who was involved in a burglary that happened a week ago, quite nearby."

"Would that be the Walkers?" prompted Julian.

"Well, yes. I'm not sure if I am meant to tell you, but as you have guessed anyway... The Inspector wants you upstairs at 4 pm for an identity parade."

"That's fine by me," said Julian. "Only it's getting a bit claustrophobic down here. As regards a solicitor, I don't have one and, quite honestly, I don't see how he could help."

"Well, Sir, if you are quite sure, only it would look bad if we had not made it plain that you are entitled to have one present."

Sergeant Wetherall then left the cell, locking the door behind him.

Shortly before 4 pm, the door opened and Sgt. Wetherall, accompanied by Adrian and Harry, entered the cell.

"You remember Harry?" asked Adrian. "He's studying law and has volunteered to help you."

"Oh, thanks," said Julian, feeling warmed by this act of friendship.

Adrian and the Sergeant withdrew leaving Julian in the hands of his new 'protector.'

"I understand you were at the Walkers'," said Harry, "only a couple of girls in the pub at lunchtime mentioned it."

"That's right," said Julian.

"Well, you seem to get about a bit. Perhaps you had better tell me what you remember."

"What's going on all of a sudden?" asked Julian. "Only one's rather shut-off down here. I thought it was just the theft of the pearls, but now we are about to have an identity parade."

"Yes, matters seem to have expanded a bit which is why Amanda was so insistent I come and see you."

"If she's so worried, why doesn't she drop the charge?"

"I think she would but it's Alfred who is so insistent. He seems to think you are some master criminal; has you down for most of the robberies in Buckinghamshire! He seems to be doing his utmost to put Amanda off you. Mind you, I understand this is typical of how he treats Amanda's boyfriends."

"Well, what's this parade about? Who's coming?"

"Julia Walker," said Harry. "From what I can gather, Alfred has been doing a bit of stirring and suggested that the Walkers should consider the possibility that you are the chap who stole from them."

"I am," said Julian.

"You what?!"

"I stole from the Walkers - nothing very much - a few trinkets plus one diamond-studded cross, but I sent it back."

"But why?" demanded Harry in disbelief.

"I just felt that a few people in the world should know how the other half live. They weren't going to miss a few bracelets or brooches, while the orphanage I grew up in is crying out for money."

"Yes, that may be, but nevertheless, you can't go around just stealing. Why didn't you just ask them for a donation or something?"

"Because people like that will object to putting a shilling in the church collection."

"Not everybody is like that," said Harry.

"Oh, I suppose not; perhaps I am giving the wrong impression, but it makes my blood boil sometimes, especially when you hear people talking at parties. They seem to think money grows on trees and only they should have the right to own a country house. Anyway, I didn't do it for myself. I gave everything away to the orphanage. At least the money went to the orphanage as anonymous gifts. I didn't want them involved in fencing the stuff. My mistake, if you can call it that, was getting them to send the cross back although I don't know how the press got hold of the story."

"Well, I'm a bit taken aback by all this. I thought you were innocent; seems to me you should just say nothing," said Harry, rather despairingly.

"I *am* innocent of the theft of the pearls," Julian insisted with an air of frustration.

"Well, I must admit, I thought you were, but mainly from what Amanda said, but if you are charged with a second theft, no one will believe you! Anyway, you'll be needed upstairs soon in the identity parade."

Harry was getting anxious; he had not expected to be defending a guilty man; on the other hand, was he guilty, and if so, of what?

"Now, the rest of the gang have agreed to be part of the line-out so at least you've got some chance of not being recognised. I think one or two of us were at the Walkers'. I wasn't and nor was Adrian, but Jeremy definitely was, and he looks a bit like you, perhaps a bit shorter, so try not to look too tall."

"I never met the Walkers," said Julian, "and I can only vaguely remember Julia. As I recall, she looked like a sister I never had, but it was quite late in the evening, in the dark and outside, so all I really got was a silhouette."

"There's hope for us yet," said Harry, gaining a little confidence and now hoping his first engagement, although unofficial, might yet prove successful.

The door opened and Inspector Rathbone entered, accompanied by Sergeant Wetherall.

"Right, I'd like you to come upstairs now, Mr Radiant. You don't need to say anything, just stand normally and you can stand wherever you like in the line."

A cheer went up when Julian appeared. However, the Inspector was quick to insist on silence. Julian said nothing but moved to place himself next to Jeremy who indeed did not look unlike himself but for his height.

Presently, Mr Victor Walker and his daughter Julia emerged and walked to the start of the line. Julia had been briefed and, coming to the end of the line, stopped then looked at each face in turn.

Julian, however, was distracted as he looked towards Mr Walker. There was something familiar about his bearing. He noticed how similar his build was to his own; allowing for twenty years or so, it could have been himself standing there thought Julian.

Mr Walker was following his daughter's progress. Eventually, she came to Julian. She looked up at him, and as she did so, she shuddered and looked back at her father. Mr Walker then looked directly at Julian who was still observing this familiar face; their eyes met and, for a moment, they both froze. Then both, slightly embarrassed, looked away pretending nothing had happened, but in truth, both were now thinking how alike they were - the same hairline, the same strong nose, and the same dimple in the jutting chin. Julia came to the end of the line and then, with the timidity of someone who expects to get a static electric shock, went back and touched Julian.

While Julian and Harry returned to the cell, the Inspector dismissed the line. "At last," he said quietly to himself, "I think we're getting somewhere."

In the cell, Harry was trying to counsel Julian.

"The Inspector is bound to ask questions about the party at the Walkers', so I suggest you say as little as possible. He will probably just be fishing. After all, the mere fact you were there does not mean you were the thief."

"I am," said Julian.

"I know, but there's no need to shout about it; the Inspector is going to need hard evidence before he can charge you."

Julian was only half listening; he was staring at the wall thinking about Mr Walker. He could be my father, he thought, but no, this was absurd. He had always understood his father had been killed in the war. Then, when he thought about it, there had been a mystery about his mother. His grandfather had always been reluctant to talk about his parents; it seemed to send him into such a fit of melancholy that on his rare visits, he always avoided the subject. It was not until his early teens that it began to matter to him, and he wished he had asked more.

"Now, is that quite clear?"

"Er, what?"

"You are not listening, are you?"

"No, I was thinking about Mr Walker. He looks so like me!"

"Well," said Harry, "I don't think a case of mistaken identity will wash with the Inspector."

Julian did not even smile. His thoughts were elsewhere. Since he had been a teenager, he had always been one step ahead, always able to think on his feet, and his ingenuity and quick thinking had managed to get him out of many a scrape, but now, his past had caught up with him. He felt hemmed in from all sides. People were telling him what to do and he did not like it; he felt depressed and alone. The trouble was he had no idea how to resolve the situation.

Harry realised he was not going to achieve very much that evening and was about to leave when Sergeant Wetherall entered.

"Ah, Sergeant, I'm leaving now."

"Very well, Sir, only Miss Charlecote is upstairs most anxious to see Mr Radiant."

Julian was jolted out of melancholy and sat up at this news.

Harry left and Sergeant Wetherall showed Amanda down to the cell.

"I'll just be outside, Miss," he said and opened the door.

Amanda entered rather timidly.

"Hello," she said. "I've come to see how you are only I can't stay.

51

Alfred said I must not see you, but I had to just say I'm sorry. I didn't mean to get you into all this trouble. It was just a game. I did not expect them to arrest you. Will you forgive me?"

"There's nothing to forgive…. Wait a minute, you mean you put the pearls in my car?"

"No, no!"

"Then who did, and anyway, you don't really think I did it do you?"

"Now, I know you didn't."

"How do you know? And in that case, why don't you withdraw the charge?"

"It's not up to me; it's Alfred. He insists you must be guilty, if not for this burglary, then the other ones in the area and you and I know, well, we know; so, I'm caught in the middle."

Julian looked at Amanda; she was clearly upset, and Julian decided there was no point in taking his frustration out on her.

"How do you know it wasn't me?" he said, challenging her.

"Because you put the rose inside the case. If you had wanted to steal them, you wouldn't have done that, there would be no point."

Julian held out his hand and took Amanda's and held it softly. Then he let go saying, "You'd better go."

"Yes," she agreed and taking a shy glance at Julian, Amanda opened the door and left.

There was a brief pause and Sergeant Wetherall entered. "Sorry to say this, but the Inspector has some more questions for you upstairs."

Julian nodded and followed the Sergeant up the stairs to the interview room.

Chapter 9

He's my father!

The interview room was cold and bare except for the table in the middle and two chairs, one at each side. The evening sunlight streamed through the window reflecting off a clock that hung on the opposite wall so beams of light made patterns across the table.

Inspector Rathbone was seated on one side puffing on a pipe. He leant back in his chair and, with his pipe in hand, signalled to Julian to sit facing him. Julian noticed he was relaxed, yet a determined unsmiling face conveyed to Julian that the Inspector was expecting a long interview.

In the short time it had taken to climb the stairs, Julian had decided that he would not give in easily. Indeed, he began to realise that if Amanda was ever going to be his, he would have to win his case and he knew that was not going to be easy. He also began to remember what Harry had said - 'The Inspector will probably just be fishing'.

The Inspector waited for Julian to relax into the chair then said slowly, "Where were you on Saturday 29th June? And I don't want to hear about books in St Albans."

"I often go fishing on Saturdays," said Julian.

"And did you go fishing that Saturday?"

Julian paused and then said quietly, "No."

"Well, where were you?"

"I think that was the day I went with a friend to Newbury Races."

"Well, we can soon check that. Name some of the horses. Constable Simpkins is keen on the horses so I'm sure he'll confirm which day it was."

"Er, Red September, Doradio, Sir Percival, oh, and The Planter; that came in at 5- 1. I was getting a bit desperate by then; I'd lost quite a lot, so saved my bacon, did The Planter; won by a short head. A friend of mine, Jeremy, had backed the other horse, which was winning all the way till it faded in the last few strides. He was really sick over that, I can tell you. Still, he'd made a bob or two earlier."

"Okay, okay; what time did you leave?"

"About 4:30 pm, I suppose."

"And what did you do then?"

Julian had anticipated this question even though his mind had been busy while he relayed his betting coup. He decided the nearer his story was to the truth, the less likely he would be tripped up.

"We stopped off at a café for tea and an iced bun then we went on to a party Jeremy had been invited to."

"Where was this party?"

"A large country house called "Whites" owned by the Walkers," said Julian very deliberately.

"Then you admit you were there then," said the Inspector with a quiver of triumph in his voice.

"Yes," said Julian nonchalantly, "and so were about 80 other people."

Julian, his spirits rising, saw his position of being proved guilty as 80-1 against, after all, the thief could be a woman. On the other hand, he had to be realistic and give the Inspector some credit and reduced the odds down to 8- 1. This figure roughly equated to the people he thought might have remotely fitted his description.

"Was the party to celebrate any particular event?"

"Not that I am aware of."

"Is Whites a big house?"

"Quite large; it has about 8 bedrooms."

"Eight? Did you count them?"

"No, I just noticed one of those old indicators in the kitchen where a bell rings if anybody needs attention."

"Did you visit any of these bedrooms?"

"Yes. Someone - I think her name was Marianne - played a few solo violin pieces and just to get away from the hubbub downstairs, we went up to this large bedroom at the back of the house."

"Were you ever alone in the room?"

"No, I don't think so."

"You didn't have occasion to notice what was in that bedroom?"

"The usual; dressing table, bed plus a large settee."

"You didn't notice any jewellery lying on the dressing table?"

"No, can't say that I did."

"Are you sure?"

"Oh, there might have been some."

"Nothing struck your eye? You didn't perhaps open the drawers or perhaps go into another bedroom?"

"No, I had no need to."

"Because you found what you wanted."

"You mean like pearl necklaces, gold earrings, or silver crosses studded with diamonds."

At this, the Inspector remained silent.

Julian was a little perturbed, he was thinking he was being clever, because he had expected the Inspector to say something about the cross and he would reply that he had read it in yesterday's paper. But now, the Inspector just sat looking at him as if he knew!

"How long have you been a thief, Mr Radiant?"

Julian was taken aback by this question. He did not expect him to be so direct. He thought if he said he wasn't, the Inspector would treat the answer with contempt. If he said he was by mentioning a time, the Inspector would still not know more than he probably already did.

"About 6 months," said Julian thoughtfully.

"And on June the 29th you stole a jewel-studded cross?"

The Inspector said this in such a calm and matter of fact way that Julian was prompted to ask,

"How do you know?"

"Because the fact that the cross was silver was not reported. You would have to have seen it to know and to open the drawer of the dressing table. The cross was not on show; it was in a bottom drawer behind several jewellery boxes and your fingerprints were found on the drawer!"

Julian suddenly found himself outwitted. He tried to think of some defence. He then remembered the inscription, *'J I am with you always, V'.*

"I was merely retrieving my property", said Julian. "The cross belonged to my mother. Mr Walker is my father."

"What?" said the Inspector. "You don't even have the same name! Now, Mr Radiant, you are going to have to do better than that."

Julian knew he was in a corner and would have to bluff his way out.

"The cross has an inscription on it - *'J I am with you always, V'.* My mother's name was Jacqueline. Anyway, allowing for the 20-plus-year age difference, didn't you notice how alike I am to Mr Walker?"

"Oh, this is preposterous," said the Inspector.

The door opened and Sergeant Wetherall popped his head round the door. "Sorry to interrupt, Sir, but there's a telephone call for you; Victor Walker, Sir."

"Talk of the devil," said the Inspector half under his breath.

"Okay, I'll take it and take Mr Radiant back to his cell. I've had more than enough charades for today."

Sergeant Wetherall took Julian back to his cell.

"Nice to be back in familiar surroundings," said Julian, slightly sarcastically.

"Tell me," said Sergeant Wetherall quietly, "why do you do it? You seem such a gentleman!"

Julian didn't bother to defend himself; it didn't seem relevant anymore.

"Well," he said, pausing for thought. "It is a question of a redistribution of wealth," he said, "a bit like Robin Hood. I am always careful not to take pieces that have sentimental value like Amanda's... I mean Miss Charlecote's pearls. I just take what will not be missed and will probably become an insurance claim and then forgotten."

"Well," said Sergeant Wetherall, "I can see the way you're thinking, but the trouble is, where do you draw the line? It would be chaos, as they say, two wrongs don't make a right. Do you play cribbage, Mr Radiant?"

"Yes, I do," said Julian with a hopeful tone in his voice as the invitation suddenly appealed to him.

"Well, I must tidy up upstairs; then I'll get us a cup of tea and come down. Sunday evening is pretty quiet round here, and the wife will be off to church, but I must lock you up first."

"I understand," said Julian.

Upstairs, Sergeant Wetherall found Inspector Rathbone muttering under his breath. "I don't believe it; I don't believe it. That Mr Walker has just withdrawn any charges! He refuses to continue with the case; he says he has got the property that matters back, that his daughter Julia was mistaken and that to continue would be too painful for all his family. It was the way he said painful for 'all' his family that made me wonder whether this Julian really is a long-lost son."

Chapter 10

A dozen white roses.

Life at Cooper's Bank had changed; there was a certain coldness in the air. Amanda felt like someone who had won the star prize in a raffle of an exotic foreign holiday and then discovered she would have to work and could not accept the prize. She had not slept well and now that it was Monday morning, the weekend seemed like a dream. Making the effort to get ready for work was difficult, but she needed to be on time. Messrs Raythorpe & Drewsnap, estate agents, were sticklers for time-keeping and indeed expected everything to be dealt with just so. Their reputation for quiet efficiency was renowned throughout Buckinghamshire. There was an important auction taking place next week and she had yet to complete a full itinerary. It was going to be a busy day. She thought it was just as well - at least she might be able to take her mind off Julian's predicament, but her pessimistic Capricorn nature soon told her otherwise. "It was all my fault, if only..." but she had said this to herself a hundred times.

Alfred, on the other hand, was busy pouring over his law books even at breakfast. He seemed to be in his element. Every now and then he would exclaim, "Ah yes, the Crown v Draper, mere belief that one had permission to enter the defendant's land was no defence. Draper was held to have been guilty of trespass."

"But I did ask him," said Amanda, realising what was behind this statement.

"You did not ask him to steal your pearls. You did not specifically say, 'Go into my bedroom'. You did not actually ask him to do anything.

He is guilty and I shall prove it!"

Amanda shrank away. She had tried to defend Julian and then attempted to create an alibi for him, but Alfred had spotted it immediately. She started to make things up and yet only made it worse. Also, if she carried on trying to make out that she had given permission, she was effectively an accomplice. If she was not careful, she would soon find herself down the road in the local jail as well. In the end, she concluded that saying nothing was probably the best course of action for now. So, she finished her breakfast, gathered her things together and drove off to town.

And so it was that while Amanda sat in her employer's office trying to concentrate on her work and failing, Julian was appearing before a magistrate and was given bail on his own security of £50, a sum which he had suddenly inherited from an unknown benefactor who had left a banker's draft at the police station for him. While there was a no note from his saviour in his hour of need, he assumed that Amanda had somehow raised the money. "Pawned the pearls," he said to himself and smiled at the irony of this possibility.

At 11:30 am, he was finally allowed to leave the custody of Her Majesty's Constabulary and return to his former life. This was going to be difficult, like trying to go back in history; the familiar landmarks he met as he drove into London failed to engender in him the feeling of comfort and stability he was looking for. On arrival at work on the Tuesday, he made excuses of sickness to his employer for his absence and then decided that, at the end of the week, he would give in his notice. He anticipated that by the time his notice had been worked, his case would be in line to be heard. This, he felt, was an easier way of dealing with the problem since to admit to involvement in theft, whether guilty or not, could have meant instant dismissal. He also realised his employer was bound to find out sooner or later, one way or another.

By Wednesday, he had realised that to try and forget about Amanda was hopeless. His mind kept wandering back to the last words she had said, "Because you put the rose inside the case". So, at lunchtime, he walked over to a florist and spent a small fortune on sending her a dozen white roses. As he strode slowly from the shop, tears came to his eyes, and he felt compelled to walk slowly down a side street to compose himself.

That evening, when the roses were delivered, Amanda was also in a melancholy mood, but having taken delivery, she closed the door and absent-mindedly unwrapped the flowers on the hall table. Her eyes focused on the note from Julian and the white petals, and she too was moved to tears and was deeply affected by this, so she hurriedly tripped up the stairs, leaving the flowers, and flew into her bedroom to sob quietly into her pillow. It was a full half an hour later that a light tap on her door was followed by Harman's deep but controlled voice saying, "I have put the flowers in water, Miss Amanda. Do you wish to have them in the sitting room or drawing room?"

"In the... in the... no, I want them up here on my dressing table, but I'll fetch them myself in a minute."

"Very well, Miss Amanda."

"It is no good," she said to herself. "I can't let things go on like this." And she resolved to go and see Inspector Rathbone the next morning and have the charges dropped notwithstanding what Alfred had said, in fact if it meant she was a conspirator to the theft, then they would have to arrest her; at least that way, she could live with herself. Besides, she thought that would upset Alfred's plans; clearly, he would not want to prove theft against Julian and her.

Amanda rose early as she wanted to see the Inspector before work; she could not spend another day in torment. She arrived at the police station at 8:30 am; Sergeant Wetherall was at the desk.

"I want to drop the charges! I shan't testify, you won't have a case,

61

you can't keep Julian here any longer, it's not fair, he only did what I told him, he didn't steal the pearls, it was my idea he stole some of my jewellery and if I ask someone to take something, that's my affair not yours"

She said all this in one explosive sentence. Sergeant Wetherall did not have a chance to interrupt.

"Ah, it's Miss Charlecote, isn't it? Well, Miss, Mr Julian was released on bail on Monday and as regards the charges, I think Inspector Rathbone would happily drop them, but for the fact that your uncle has filed charges of theft of some papers of his, some house deeds or other documents, so you see, it is out of your hands now! But I must say I don't remember a case before where I felt the accused was being unfairly persecuted. He may be a bit of a lad, but in truth, he seems a gentleman to me, Miss. The whole time he was here, he showed proper respect. In fact, we spent a few pleasant hours together chatting and playing cribbage and in all that time, I did not detect any feeling that he was what you might call one of the 'criminal classes'. Perhaps I should not admit this, Miss, but it seems to me Mr Radiant hardly had any time in which to steal the pearls, never mind find some of Mr Charlecote's papers, and what would he want with them? It doesn't tie in with the previous thefts - they have all been for jewellery or small valuable objects. But there it is; unless your uncle suddenly finds these deeds and withdraws this further charge, there is not a lot I can do about it. Sorry, Miss."

Amanda turned slowly on her heels and walked out of the police station. "Alfred," she said to herself, "what is he up to?" He had not said anything about these deeds. What deeds anyway, and why did he suddenly feel so sure that Julian had taken them and then add this to the charges against him? What was going on?

After a day's work, Amanda arrived back at Cooper's Bank at about 5.45 pm and went straight into the study where she expected to find

Alfred. She was not disappointed; with law books scattered across the desk, he sat mumbling to himself.

"Ah there you are! Discovered any more lost papers? Someone pinched some of your briefs? How about your life assurance policy? I should check on that if I were you. You could be in need of it! He may be a thief, but you are conducting a personal vendetta and this time, I'm going to see you don't win. I shall perjure myself and give Julian an alibi."

"Oh, I suppose you are upset about the extra charge, but that's just a means to an end. The point is you and I know he is the jewel thief, and it is just a question of time before I shall prove it. Anyway, I need this case to establish myself; cases like this get a lot of publicity. He'll only get about a year, or two. I don't need your evidence; there were so many witnesses to the events of you shouting from the top of the stairs that Julian had stolen your pearls. I don't need to call you as a witness."

Amanda clenched her fists and gritted her teeth, beaten again, at least for now. So, she left the study and just outside, she found Mary, the girl who came in to do the cleaning.

"Excuse me, Miss Amanda, only I found this. I think it could be important; they look like curls of hair tied with small ribbons."

"My mother's and grandmother's hair! Oh thanks, I thought I had lost them."

"Oh right, only I found them when I was cleaning."

"That's great, Mary, thanks; have you finished for the day?"

"Yes, I'll be going now, bye."

Mary left and Amanda followed her, wishing her goodnight as she showed her out of the front door.

In the background, they could hear Alfred suddenly shout, "That's it! Got him at last! I can prove he was in the bedroom and took the pearls, aha!"

Amanda, on the other hand, was even more worried about what he had discovered now, as she knew Julian hadn't taken the pearls, but how could she prove it? She turned the matter over in her mind and came to the same conclusion as the Inspector. If someone else had taken them, they would have to have timed their actions to take into account Julian's movements; otherwise, they would have bumped into him. Someone would have to have decided not only to steal the pearls, but to know Julian would be doing the same thing; it was ridiculous. After all, no one knew that Julian was even going to be at the party till about six o'clock, except of course Harman, Diana and Alfred. 'Alfred… it's got to be Alfred; he is the only one who actually knows where I keep them and I think he probably knows where I hang the key, up behind my mother's picture, and has worked it out like Julian did. Yet he can't possibly hope to prove someone else stole something he actually stole himself,' thought Amanda to herself. She churned the facts over in her mind again and again. Something was missing, some fact which would prove Julian was innocent and someone else guilty. Amanda's mood had changed; she was now resolved to meet up with Julian and see if together they could work it out, but then she suddenly realised she did not actually know where Julian lived! "Ah!" she said to herself. "Sergeant Wetherall may know."

The next day, she strode into the police station and, hardly pausing, said to the constable on duty, "Can I please have the address of Mr Julian Radiant?"

"Well, and you are?"

"Miss Amanda Charlecote."

"Are you related or perhaps his solicitor?"

"Neither; just a friend."

"Well," said the constable, "I regret that I am not at liberty to give out his address. Sorry, love, but it is the rules."

'Stymied again,' thought Amanda, and quietly but slowly she walked out of the police station and off to work.

Chapter 11

Out of the
mouths of babes

About two weeks later, Amanda was sitting in the kitchen drinking a cup of coffee when she heard a knock at the front door. She was not expecting anybody and did not think Alfred would want any calls. Her curiosity got the better of her and, rather than wait till Harman opened the door, she went herself.

Standing there was an old man who looked slightly agitated. He was slim and tall and although slightly stooped, even to her untrained eye, he had a certain familiarity about his looks.

"Good evening, Mademoiselle. I am looking for Monsieur Walker; is he here?"

"Oh no, this is Cooper's Bank; you want Whites. It is about 10 miles the other side of town."

"Alors," he mumbled to himself. "Quelle route est-ce? I ask, which road?" he said.

"The Aylesbury Road," said Amanda.

"Ah, merci bien… thank you."

A taxi was behind him in the road and the driver leant out of the window. "Is this it, mate, or are we off again? Only this is costing you a packet."

"Un moment, un moment please," said the man impatiently and slightly breathlessly.

"Have you travelled far, Sir?" asked Amanda.

"Oh, from Pérouges near Lyons," he said.

"You mean Lyons in France?!"

"Oui, Mademoiselle, only it is most urgent I see Mr Walker. I feel, I feel, responsible." He said the last word with difficulty in a manner that implied guilt rather than any problem over translation. 'He must be nearly eighty,' thought Amanda.

"Can I offer you some refreshment, Sir? You could telephone Mr Walker from here."

"You know the number?"

"Oh yes, I know his daughter Julia."

"He has a daughter; I know not this."

He leant heavily against the door struggling with himself over what to do.

"Are you sure you won't come in and rest awhile? said Amanda, seeing the gentleman was becoming more distressed by the minute.

"Ah, you are so kind, Mademoiselle. Perhaps a glass of water..."

"I'm sure we can manage coffee or something stronger if you prefer."

The taxi driver, by now realising his fare was not going to return to the cab until he was sure of his way, had got out and walked up to Amanda.

"Do you know this gentleman, Miss? Only I have been driving him around for hours. Never quite seems to know where he is going and there is three pounds, five shillings on the clock already."

"Well," said Amanda, "I know the Walkers; they're about 10 miles towards Aylesbury."

"Well, that sounds hopeful at least."

"But now I come to think of it, I believe they have gone away and won't be back for a couple of days."

"In that case, I had better take you to a hotel, mate," said the taxi driver, speaking directly to the gentleman.

"Si seulement je savais où était Julian," said the gentleman to himself.

The taxi driver did not take much notice of this statement, but Amanda's mouth dropped open in surprise.

"Vous sais Julian? Julian Radiant?" said Amanda in her best French.

"Oui, Mademoiselle, et vous?"

"Yes, he was here about 10 days ago only I don't know where he is now," said Amanda feeling slightly silly when she said this.

"But is he okay… is he arrêté?"

"No, they released him on bail."

The taxi driver was intrigued by this conversation, but then interrupted; "Are we going to a hotel or not?"

"Are you Monsieur Ragiant?" asked Amanda.

"Why yes, Mademoiselle!"

"Then I need to talk to you; would you like to stay the night?"

"I could not, oh no, it is too much."

"But I must talk to you about Julian, only he did not do it, he is not guilty, I mean, well, please stay, Monsieur Ragiant, and then I can explain it all to you."

By this time, Harman had become puzzled by the commotion at the front door and had walked over. From the entrance hall, his deep voiced sounded; "Can I be of assistance, Miss Amanda?"

"Yes, Harman, you can get Monsieur Ragiant's bags from the taxi. We have a guest for the night."

"Did you say Monsieur Ragiant?"

"Yes," said Amanda.

"Is this wise?" asked Harman who had quickly guessed there must be some connection with this infamous Julian.

"Yes, very wise," said Amanda whose Capricorn glare froze even the dour Harman temporarily to the spot.

"Now, Monsieur, if you would like to pay this gentleman your fare… Do you have some English money?"

"Oh, oui, but are you sure I do not intrude upon you?"

"Not at all; you will be doing me a favour," said Amanda "I need to talk to you as I want to find out about Julian."

"Ah, very well then, this is most kind of you." As he said this, he counted pound notes into the hand of the taxi driver who, in turn, ferreted around in his pockets for the change from £4.00.

Amanda led Mr Ragiant through the hall into the drawing room and escorted him to an armchair.

"Let me get you something to drink; café?"

"Oh oui, thank you."

"Have you eaten today?" asked Amanda who now saw how tired and frail this man really was as he sank into the armchair.

"I had a little bread and pâté I'd bring with me."

"Then if you'll excuse me a moment, I'll get the coffee and ask Harman to set an extra place for dinner. We usually eat about seven; is that okay for you?"

"Oh, this is very kind of you, very kind."

Amanda left to speak to Harman who had strangely mellowed a little.

"I expected he would want dinner; he looked very tired. It's just that if I'm not warned and then things get behind, Mr Alfred holds me responsible."

"Well, tonight I expect he will have his dinner in his study so there's no great rush. I've never said this before," said Amanda, "but, well Harman, you must find it difficult sometimes taking your orders from me or Alfred since my parents died; I hope we don't put you out too often."

"Strange to say, Miss, I can usually cope with your wishes, even if there are a few surprises shall we say, but it's Mr Alfred never making up his mind and then saying he said so and so all the time. Now that really upsets me."

"Thanks, Harman. Now, we need some coffee, but don't worry, I'll make it. However, could you do me a favour?"

"What's that, Miss Amanda?"

"Well, actually, it may save you a problem later. Could you go and ask if Alfred is going to have his dinner in his study, only put it in such a way that you assume he will? It's just that I'd like to talk to Mr Ragiant without Alfred knowing he's here."

"I'll see what I can do, Miss."

"Great!" said Amanda. She had soon made the coffee and backed through the kitchen door carrying the tray. Amanda arrived back in the drawing room to find Monsieur Ragiant fast asleep. She smiled and placed the tray on a table near the window. She then took a cushion and gently placed it under Monsieur Ragiant's head to save him from getting a crick in his neck. She then lifted his feet gently onto a footstool and laid a rug across him. Once she was finished, she returned to the kitchen to find Harman and tell him there was no hurry for dinner as far as she and Monsieur Ragiant were concerned. Harman, in the meantime, confirmed that Mr Alfred would indeed be eating in his study.

It was nearly an hour before Monsieur Ragiant awoke. "The coffee won't be a moment," said Amanda, deliberately, pretending that he had only drifted off for a few minutes.

"Oh, pardon, merci."

"It's okay; just rest a moment. How long have you been travelling?"

"Since five this morning."

"Well, I suggest you retire after we have eaten and then we can talk in the morning when you are refreshed, only there is so much I want to ask you."

Amanda then fetched fresh coffee which they drank almost in silence, then she showed Monsieur Ragiant into the dining room where Harman served dinner. The Frenchman ate the roast pork with relish but declined the sweet in favour of a little cheese with biscuits.

Peter Gatenby

When he had clearly finished, Amanda showed him to his room.

The next day being Monday, Amanda rose early. She wanted, if possible, to avoid any problem with Alfred who still did not know they had a guest. But she need not have worried. Alfred had risen early, and, after only a cup of coffee, had left to go into town to the library where he wanted to consult some more law books.

When Monsieur Ragiant emerged, he apologised to Harman for being late. Harman assured the gentleman it was no trouble to him and that he was not in any way late. Then Monsieur Ragiant looked at his watch and the hall clock and realised he was still running on French time, which is an hour earlier and he visibly relaxed, although still felt he was intruding. Amanda, however, came to the rescue. She took him by the hand and led him into the dining room. "Ah, merci ma chèrie," he said and sighed as he thought how alike his daughter Amanda was.

"Did you sleep well?" she asked.

"Yes, thank you," he said.

They ate breakfast slowly and quietly and when they had nearly finished, Amanda, perhaps without thinking too clearly, said, "Julian gave me the impression you had died some years ago when he was about 12".

"Yes, that was my fault, you see, I was very ill and I was expected to die, but when I recovered many months later, I got to thinking that it was better Julian should think I had died and grow up as an English boy rather than half English and half French; besides, his father always promised to look after him, but it seems he did no more than provide some money and then only to the orphanage rather than to Julian himself. So, when Julian really needed a father, neither he nor I were there. Now I must put things right and this is why I must get to the Walkers' house and find out what has occurred."

Amanda remained silent for a while at this last remark and then, plucking up courage again, she asked, "Am I right in thinking your daughter was Julian's mother?"

"That is right, my dear."

"And she died in the war then?"

"Yes. It was a most terrible thing, if only she had not come back. She did it for me, you see; she thought I would be in trouble, but I had taken precautions, she need not have returned, but when she did, she fell straight into the Hands of the Germans. She was shot as a member of the Maquis."

"And was she?" Amanda asked.

"Oh yes, she had obtained vital information about Operation Sea Lion by passing as a German maid, she spoke fluent German because she had a German cousin and often went to stay with her before the war. When she returned, landing by parachute with two British officers, she was arrested. I believe she tried to bluff her way out by pretending to be a German who had infiltrated the British Secret Service, but the Gestapo were suspicious after seeing her go into our local school. So, after showing them a photograph, they got the children to tell them everything they knew about my daughter. The children did not know what they were doing. "This is Mademoiselle Jacquie, she is our teacher, she is nice to us, she has always been at our teacher, is she coming back?" Oh dear; 'out of the mouths of babes' I think the English say. She was shot the next morning while the two British officers, because they were in uniform, were not treated as spies but were still sent to a prisoner-of-war camp."

There was a pause while Amanda took in all this new information, then slowly, and almost thinking out loud, she said, "Then Julian's mother must have come to England, met Julian's father, given birth and then gone back to France where she died; but why come to England in the first place?"

"It was Victor, Victor Walker. He had got trapped behind enemy lines with a badly injured friend. They stayed with us hoping his friend would recover but he died. By that time, my Jacquie had fallen in love with the handsome Captain Walker and was expecting his child. It was thought best if she went to England to give birth. Also, it meant she could deliver vital information in person, so they made their way to St. Malo and managed to take a small fishing boat across La Manche at night. Julian was born in Victor Walker's own house and stayed until he was about seven months old. Then, because of being worried about me and the fact that the British were putting pressure on her to get more of the Germans' plans, she agreed to parachute back into France. Julian was put into the orphanage by his father because he was called back to his unit himself. I believe he never actually told his own parents that Julian was his son. I do not think they approved of my Jacquie."

Amanda listened quietly to all this and then said, "I am beginning to see how Julian must feel rather isolated with no real family of his own."

They finished breakfast and then Amanda rang the Walkers. "Oh, you are there, only I have a Frenchman here called Monsieur Ragiant and he is anxious to talk to Mr Walker."

Amanda had been talking to Mrs Walker but there was a distinct pause and then she asked, "French, did you say?"

"Yes," said Amanda.

"And what did you say his name was? Wasn't that Julian fellow called Ragiant?"

"Nearly," said Amanda. "Radiant, actually, but he is Julian's grandfather. Julian just changed his name slightly!"

"Well, what does he want?"

"Well, I'm not sure, but he seems to feel he should talk to Mr Walker."

There was a long pause while Mrs Walker went off to speak to her husband. Eventually, she came back saying he would need to be at the Walkers within the next hour as they would be away for the rest of the day.

Amanda said that would be fine even though she knew she would be a bit late for work. However, rather than ring her employer with an excuse now, she decided to make her excuses when she eventually arrived, whenever that might be! So, she got the car out and having seated Mr Ragiant in the back, drove off to Whites arriving thirty minutes later. She then escorted Mr Ragiant into the Walkers' residence. The door was opened by Mrs Walker who seemed somewhat put out but said very little. Showing Mr Ragiant into a small front sitting room, she said that Mr Walker would be with him very shortly.

Amanda realised that whatever Julian's grandfather wanted to say to Mr Walker, he would probably prefer to speak to him on his own and thus made an excuse saying that there was something she needed to say to Julia, the Walkers' daughter, and she left Mr Ragiant to meet with Mr Walker in peace.

Julia greeted Amanda with a secretive grin and whisked her outside into the garden on that fortunately warm, sunny morning.

"Do you know what this is all about?" quizzed Julia.

Amanda said, "I don't know the whole story, but I am under the impression that it had something to do with the war and Julian's father."

Amanda stopped short of saying that she assumed Julian was actually her half-brother for fear of making mischief if she was wrong. Julia told Amanda that her mother was acting very strangely and basically told her to keep out of the way while Mr Ragiant, or whatever his name was, was here. The girls then realised they were outside the room where the meeting was taking place but could not be seen because of a large rambling rose bush and, although they could hear voices and every now and then a few French words, they could only catch a few phrases of what was being said, but also got the impression that Mr Ragiant was becoming increasingly upset. Then it was obvious that

Mrs Walker had entered the room and the discussions, if you could call them that, came to an abrupt end.

Amanda looked at Julia. "I think I had better go and rescue poor Mr Ragiant. I'll let you know later in the week what I find out." Then the two girls tiptoed round to the back door so that Amanda could appear in the hall as if by accident.

"Are you okay, Mr Ragiant?" she said to the old man almost in a whisper. "Non, je regret!" came the reply. He was clearly annoyed and a little shaken at his treatment. "But I have Julian's place of residence," he said, "so I must go and see him." With this, the old man took a deep breath as if to pump new life into his aged frame and walked towards the front door.

They drove back to Cooper's Bank almost in silence. Eventually, Amanda asked where Julian lived. "I have the address here; it is a place called Highgate in North London. I believe I can get there by train," he said. "Would you be so kind as to take me to a station where I might get a train?"

"Certainly," she said. "Do you wish to go now? It's just that I should be at work, so I could drop you off on the way, once you have collected your baggage."

"Oh, I must go now, I think; that would be most kind of you."

Amanda drove up to Cooper's Bank and then insisted Mr Ragiant had some coffee before departing as she could see him not stopping before he eventually got to Julian's place. She then took him to the station and stayed to see him safely into the carriage. The old man said, 'au revoir' and, taking her by the hand, kissed it. "Maybe I see you again soon," he said, "with Julian perhaps."

Amanda was touched by this, although, at this stage, all Amanda could see was her appearing in a court room with Julian as the accused. Amanda smiled and said she hoped Julian would look after him, then, placing one of her visiting cards into his hand. she said," Write to me, won't you?" feeling that this might suggest to Mr Ragiant that he was not alone, but had someone he could call upon.

Back at Raythorpe & Drewsnap, it was gone 12 noon before Amanda eventually put in an appearance, however, although armed with an excuse about her car playing up and then running out of petrol, she did not need it as no one seemed to think she was late. Her diary still showed she had an appointment with a new client, who had actually rung her very late on Friday to say that he could not come that morning, but would come on Tuesday instead. Amanda's diary did not reflect this change. So, having realized why there was no interrogation, she pretended that the customer had kept her talking so long on the delights of where they were moving to that she needed to go back on Tuesday morning to complete the details of the sale.

Over the next three weeks, Amanda's routine returned to normal, or as normal as it could be with Adrian at home and various cronies of his calling. During this time, she plucked up enough courage to pen a few lines to Julian, finishing it with 'love Amanda' and sketching a picture of a white rose. She was becoming both concerned and disappointed not to have received a reply after the best part of a month, when she received two letters, on neither of which she recognized the handwriting. One of them had a French stamp which she guessed was from Mr Ragiant. The letter was written in a mixture of English and French - 'franglais' she thought to herself. Mr R had seen Julian and said that she, Amanda, must have been of some good influence as he seemed to be more grown up and contrite than he expected and was pleased that Julian had promised from now on he would be following an honest career. There was no mention of what this was to be; indeed, in the end, it seemed Julian had convinced the old man that he would be okay. He finished his letter by ladling praises on her for the assistance she had given him, as well as asking her to thank Harman and Mr Alfred for making a stranger so welcome.

Having digested all this, she opened the other letter which she was pleased to see was from Julian. It started very formally with 'Dear Miss Amanda Charlecote' as if trying to distance himself from her, but as the letter progressed, it moved from a strange apology for all the trouble he had caused to a few phrases that seemed almost in code. He mentioned her Capricorn trait of instinctively knowing what was right and hoped the future would include him, and yet, and in case this was too presumptuous, he added 'as a friend'. He then finished off with 'Love Julian' and finally a PS which made Amanda smile; 'Perhaps this is not the time to broach anything further'!

Julian, meanwhile, had taken a job as a junior clerk in a firm of architects. He had been asked why the change from stockbroker. He explained he had always wanted to study to become an architect, which was not untrue; indeed, he had done about half a year of the first year's study for the professional exams. He made out he just needed money to tide him over while he studied. At this stage, he did not formally have a criminal record and figured that should he suddenly become a person of ill repute, as junior clerk, he could easily leave without much fuss. However, the firm was most helpful, and, with encouragement from other clerks, he decided he had better join the evening class they were all going to. Thus, he was settling into a new life, when, out of the blue, the reality of the situation was brought back into focus by a telephone call from Harry, who seemed to know that a summons was in the post to appear before a magistrate to be formally charged with theft. Sure enough, he received a summons the next day to appear at Aylesbury magistrates' court to answer the charge of theft. Harry had said this was not a formal trial and therefore to say as little as possible. Julian, therefore, asked for a day off without giving any reason for his need of a holiday.

The following Friday, he duly appeared at court. It was a brief hearing where all he had to do was answer his name and give an address then he was bound over to appear at the local crown court a month hence when the trial would formally take place.

Chapter 12

The Crown versus Radiant

It was a rather dull early autumn day when Julian drove up to Aylesbury to appear for trial at the Crown Court. He had managed to wangle a week's holiday without too many questions being asked. He felt the trial could not last any longer and either he would be disappointing his new employers with his resulting non-appearance or be back a free man! Nobody queried the fact that his week's holiday started on a Thursday, but that had been the day set for the trial to start.

Harry met him at the Court entrance and took him into a room reserved for the accused and his counsel. Unbeknown to Julian, Harry had seen this as a chance to do a bit of extra study and had been going through the evidence he had been presented with.

They had about an hour to chat before they were formally called to appear, by which time a jury had been selected and sworn in. The judge asked both defence and prosecution if they objected to any of the jurors. Julian made no objection while Alfred scowled at a couple of faces trying to decide if they had been at the party, but in the end, also did not make any objection. He felt that if he did raise an objection, he would look a bit silly before he started if it turned out they had nothing to do with any party.

Judge Albert Wentworth then queried Julian's defence counsel saying he was entitled to be formally represented and if he could not afford such counsel, the court would pay. Julian said he was quite happy with the current arrangement, quietly wishing the whole matter would be over as quickly as possible. The judge then turned to Mr Alfred Charlecote and was somewhat surprised by the fact that the prosecution was also the aggrieved party. Mr Charlecote said that on the same basis that the defendant could represent himself, so could the plaintiff. The judge acknowledged this but said he had never come across a case quite like this. Alfred then, knowing the press were present, said loudly, "Too many burglaries have taken place locally and someone must put a stop to it and if I must take on that burden, so be it." This grandstanding speech was quickly brought to a close by the judge wanting to ensure his court was not going to be made into some stage production. "Mr Charlecote, at this stage, I would ask you to be brief; after all, we have not even called the first witness or laid out the charges."

The mood in the court was measurably changed by this exchange from one of quiet attention to everybody pricking up their ears and murmurings of 'what's this all about'!

The judge asked the clerk to read out the charge which he did.

"Julian Victor Radiant, you are charged that on 7th July 1962, you did steal a double string of pearls and also deeds of a property known as Cooper's Bank in the county of Buckinghamshire contrary to law. How do you plead?"

Julian rose to acknowledge the charge and said very deliberately, "Not guilty, your Honour."

The judge then turned to Mr Charlecote, "You may call your first witness".

Alfred could have called Amanda, but deliberately wanted to show the theft was the last in a series of thefts in Buckinghamshire and knew Inspector Rathbone would be the person to enlighten the court.

"I call Inspector Rathbone of Aylesbury CID."

The Inspector walked to the witness stand and was sworn in.

Alfred turned to him slowly as if savouring the hors d'oeuvre of a carefully prepared meal.

"Inspector, could you tell the court how you came to be at Cooper's Bank, on 7th July at about 11:45 in the evening?"

"I was attending the premises as I expected a theft may take place that evening."

"You actually expected a theft to take place? Was this pure serendipity or did you have some previous knowledge or event that made you suspicious that a crime may be committed?" asked Alfred, hoping the Inspector would elaborate. He was not disappointed as Inspector Rathbone continued.

"There have been a number of thefts of jewellery from large country houses in Buckinghamshire in recent months and one of my constables advised me that he thought there was to be a party at Cooper's Bank on the evening of 7th July. I believed that many university students would be returning home that day for the summer break. Constable Simpkins has a younger brother at university and hence the information was passed on to me. Bearing in mind all the thefts seemed to be at similar gatherings, I had attended Cooper's Bank earlier that day to warn the occupants of the possibility of them being targeted."

Alfred was a little surprised at this as Amanda had not mentioned it. He just knew a constable would be placed in mufti to keep his eyes and ears open. However, the fact that the Inspector had actually deemed to attend himself leant weight to the gravity of the expected crime and he began to delight in the Inspectors description which was setting the scene almost without Alfred needing to prompt him.

"How long were you at Cooper's Bank in the morning, Inspector?"

"Only about ten minutes, but I did meet Miss Amanda Charlecote and, of course, the accused."

"You actually met the accused that morning, Inspector?"

"Yes, and he fitted the description of the person we were looking for precisely!"

Alfred had to stop himself from almost springing into the air as this last fact was revealed.

"You mean you already had a suspect for these earlier thefts?"

"Yes. He had to be a young person who would fit in with a young crowd, but probably not a university student as not only would his name then be known by others, but also some of these thefts took place when most students were away at university. Our break came when an honest citizen, a nun, as it happened, advised us that she had been asked to return certain property, apparently on the basis that it had been stolen in error. Now, for a seasoned jewel thief to admit this, I must say, it seemed rather strange to me, however, we had the note and a handwriting expert gave us a little more to go on in determining the type of person we were looking for."

"So can you outline the description of the person you were seeking in connection with all the thefts in Buckinghamshire, Inspector?"

"From various witness statements, we concluded that we were looking for a young athletic man, about 6 feet tall, dark, reasonably well educated and probably someone who had a car."

"Does the accused fit this description?"

"Precisely," said the Inspector.

"So, when you met Mr Radiant on the morning of 7th July, why did not arrest him or at least take him to the police station for questioning?"

"Well, I must admit I had thought of questioning the accused, but he was alibied by Miss Amanda Charlecote at that time, but I felt we had our man and all I had to do was to catch him red-handed."

Alfred was just thinking this was so easy but took a step back when he heard he was alibied by Amanda.

"Alibied by Amanda... I mean, Miss Charlecote? I thought they had only met that day."

"In truth, that may be the case, but she advised that an aunt of hers had given him a bed for the night at a time when the previous theft had taken place, and, not wishing to argue the point, I let the matter go."

Alfred was quick to turn this last fact to his advantage.

"So, you think this alibi may have been false then."

"I am pretty sure now, from what I have learnt since."

"And what would that be, Inspector?"

"Mr Radiant admitted to me that he had stolen a diamond-encrusted silver cross."

At this point, His Honour Judge Wentworth stopped the proceedings to ask the Inspector a question; "The theft of a cross is not on the charge sheet; why is that?"

"Well, your Honour, the owner refused to formally register the theft or make any kind of charge against the accused."

"I see," said the judge. "Did other people who have had goods stolen come forward to make a formal statement?"

"We had a couple, but it seems that as soon as they got the insurance claim paid, they did not want the trouble of appearing in court."

The judge then turned towards Alfred. "It seems you are indeed acting as a good citizen, Mr Charlecote; you may continue."

Alfred positively glowed with this last accolade handed to him by the judge. He now felt he was unstoppable and that single-handedly, he was about to bring a crime wave to an end.

"Inspector, you say Mr Radiant admitted stealing this silver cross, but how does this relate to matters regarding the alibi?"

"Because the cross was stolen on the night he was meant to be staying with this aunt. Indeed, Miss Amanda made out that Mr Radiant was some kind of long-lost cousin whose character was beyond reproach."

The judge, almost as if he had been too kind to the prosecution and wanted to level the playing field, interjected, "Inspector, please keep your answers strictly to the point. Miss Amanda is not on trial here."

"My apologies, your Honour."

Alfred continued - he did not want to lose the advantage, so he quickly moved to the evening.

"Inspector, can you describe what happened that evening when you arrested Mr Radiant?"

"It was perhaps fortunate that I decided to go that evening. I arrived quite late, but had made provision for one of my detectives, Detective Constable Green, to be, as it were, a guest at the party, to observe and see if he could spot the jewellery thief. I was pretty sure it was Mr Radiant, but was hoping to catch him in the act, so to speak."

"And did you catch him in the act?"

"Well, almost. As I arrived, Miss Amanda Charlecote shouted from the top of the stairs, "Julian, you thief, you stole my pearls!" or words very close to that."

"What happened then?"

"I grabbed Mr Radiant and got him to empty his pockets there and then."

"Did you find the pearls?"

"Not immediately."

"Please explain, Inspector; you say, 'not immediately'."

"Well, he did not have the pearls on him, but they were found a little later by Constable Simpkins in the glove compartment of his car."

"Were any fingerprints found on the case the pearls were in?"

"Yes, Mr Radiant's and some we have not managed to identify."

"Were these other prints Miss Amanda's?"

"No, our fingerprint expert said they were most likely a man's."

Alfred did not want to hear this and realised his questioning was going awry. He had expected the Inspector to just say yes, they were Amanda's; now a small doubt had been sown in the minds of the jury. He needed to gain the upper ground. So, quickly, he said to the judge, "That is all the questions I have for this witness."

The judge turned to Julian who, although quietly sitting on his own, had been prepped by Harry. "Do you wish to question this witness, Mr Radiant?"

"Yes," said Julian and leapt to his feet and moved across the courtroom to face the Inspector.

A murmur of approval came from the public gallery where Adrian and others who had been at the party were sitting. They now knew, or at least were fairly sure that Julian was being harshly treated and, from what Amanda had told Adrian, had not actually stolen the pearls. So, they were willing Julian to score a few points of his own.

"Inspector did you see me come down the main stairs from Miss Amanda's bedroom?"

"No," said the Inspector.

"Then how do you know I had been upstairs?"

"Because several witnesses told us that they saw you descend the stairs shortly before I arrested you."

"How long do you think it was between the time I came down these stairs and when you grabbed me by the arm?"

"Going by the information gleaned from several witnesses and Miss Amanda, I would have thought no more than three or four minutes."

"Did you find the pearls in my possession then when you stopped me?"

"No."

"Then when and how do you think I managed to steal the pearls?"

"I assume you must have gone down the backstairs, placed the pearls in the glove compartment of your car and then gone back up to come down the main stairs to be confronted by me and Miss Amanda of course."

"What did you find when I emptied my pockets onto the table in the hall?"

"About three pounds in cash, a white handkerchief and a small box with a brooch in it."

85

"Who did the brooch belong to?"

"Miss Amanda."

"This brooch is not on the charge sheet; why is that?"

Julian was becoming more confident and said this in a similar manner to the judge querying the absence of the silver cross from the charge sheet.

The Inspector paused and then, feeling a little foolish, said,

"It was apparently agreed that you could take it; some kind of game between you and Miss Amanda."

A distinct 'yes' was heard from the gallery. The judge scowled in that direction, but as there was no further outburst, he let it go.

"Do you not think it is strange that I apparently stole the pearls, went down the back stairs, placed them in the glove pocket of my car and then, instead of driving off into the sunset, came back to the scene of the supposed crime, then walked down the main stairs still with some of my ill-gotten gains in my pocket? Why should I do all that and still have something in my pocket to incriminate myself?"

The judge then interjected, "Mr Radiant, please be careful to question the witness rather than making a statement or hoping to elicit an opinion".

"Well," said Julian, "I am being accused of putting the pearls in my car. Am I not allowed to question this? The prosecution raised the matter."

"That is true, but the correct procedure is to ask a question. However, in the circumstances, I will allow the Inspector to answer."

The Inspector answered in a rather thoughtful tone: "I must admit this aspect of the case has always puzzled me. It did seem you had very little time to go up to the bedroom and yet come down and up the back stairs and then descend the main stairs and get talking to a certain Jane Lawrence and all in the space of not more than fifteen minutes."

"Inspector Rathbone, I am charged with stealing some property deeds; have these been found?"

"No, we have not been able to ascertain where these might be."

"Have you searched my car?"

"Yes."

"Have you searched anywhere else?"

"We did make a search of the grounds around Cooper's Bank in case you may have hidden them to retrieve later but found nothing."

The judge had himself forgotten about the theft of these property deeds being on the charge sheet, and, turning to Alfred Charlecote, said," Mr Charlecote. do you intend to raise this aspect of your case? After all, even from my viewpoint I am struggling to see any connection."

"It is a question of circumstances, your Honour. They were in my study before this theft took place and not afterwards. I have therefore added it to the list of missing property."

The judge looked slightly cross at this admission. "Am I to understand that it may just be coincidence that these property documents have gone missing? What exactly are we talking about?"

Alfred had foreseen this although he hoped to avoid too many questions as it was his "holding charge" to ensure Amanda was not able to persuade the police to drop the other charge, and so he handed the judge a copy of a mortgage deed.

The judge looked at the document and was still puzzled over why a jewel thief should now be ferreting about a study which was presumably elsewhere in the house other than in a bedroom. "Has the accused seen a copy of this, Mr Charlecote?" he asked.

"Eh, no."

Alfred then looked through his papers and, in the end, reluctantly passed his own copy to Julian.

Julian saw that it was a copy of a deed with a revenue stamp on the top giving proof that the stamp duty had been paid, but rather than read the front, he turned over several pages at once and started reading there.

'To my brother, Alfred Charlecote, I leave all my stocks and shares outlined in the attached list marked A and furthermore, I leave in trust all my house, Cooper's Bank, and attached estate outlined in the title deeds to be held in trust for my daughter Amanda, until she be both married and be over age 21 when she shall take possession '

Julian thought to himself, 'So, that's why Alfred is so against Amanda's boyfriends. He's going to lose his house as soon as she gets married'. Julian was quick to realise that Alfred would not want any of these facts to be mentioned and indeed, he must hope he just proves the theft of the pearls. So, turning back to the Inspector, he said, "Thank you, Inspector", and returned to his seat.

The judge was also becoming concerned at what was beginning to look like a witch hunt and he glanced at the clock. Time had drifted on during all the evidence from the Inspector and he had allowed this to continue after the normal lunch break. As he was conscious that the Inspector would have more important crimes to investigate than this one, he brought matters to a close. "I am adjourning this case for today, but I want to see both parties in my chambers first."

The judge rose and exited followed by Alfred and Julian.

'What's this about?' wondered Julian. Had he committed some contempt of court? However, as soon as they entered the judge's chambers, it soon became apparent that it was not Julian the judge was becoming frustrated with but Alfred.

"Mr Charlecote, as a practising barrister, I would have thought you would have examined the evidence for the charges very closely. So far, we have little motive or even opportunity for Mr Radiant here to have committed the offence he has been charged with and before you tell me he is guilty of several previous thefts, may I remind you that he has not been charged with them. As for these missing deeds, unless you come up with some strong evidence of their being stolen rather than merely being mislaid, I suggest you drop that from the charge by Friday morning. Do you have other witnesses who will resolve the charge of theft of these pearls?"

"Yes, your Honour. I have a witness who will bring considerable weight to bear on the case of the theft."

"Very well; I can't say I am happy with this. I feel if the evidence had been tested under the new proposed system, it would have been most unlikely that a case would have been brought. Until 10:00 am tomorrow then."

Alfred left the room with his tail between his legs, realising that Julian had been far cannier than he had expected with his questions about the time available to commit the crime, as well as raising the matter of the deeds which he thought would be forgotten about.

Julian was allowed to stay in a nearby hotel on his surety that he would not leave the premises which was covered by the £50 already bonded.

So it was that at about 2:15pm, Julian found himself in the hotel with a constable nearby but was allowed to talk to Harry who was full of smiles when he greeted him. "I think we may have got him."

"Who?" asked Julian, a little confused.

"Mr Alfred Charlecote", he said. "I have been going through his list of witnesses and he is going to call Mary Downing who is the girl who cleans for the Charlecotes. So, I asked her why she thought she was being called. Turns out she found two curls of hair tied with small coloured ribbons; she said they were apparently in the box where the pearls were kept."

"They were," said Julian. "I remember seeing them. I assumed they must be from her mother and grandmother, but how does that help us?"

"Well, when she told me where she had found them, I nearly fell off my chair. Guess where they were!"

"Well, I don't know, in Amanda's bedroom, I suppose."

"No, in Alfred's bedroom."

"What? That can't be right; it would mean that someone took the pearls into his room and opened the box allowing the hair to fall out. Are you sure she is right?"

"I questioned her very carefully on this and she said it must have been Mr Alfred's room because it was the Tuesday after the party; she works Tuesdays and Fridays, and she always does Mr Alfred on Tuesday and Miss Amanda on Friday. However, she thinks he heard her outside his study a few weeks ago, but at the time, she did not mention where she had found the hair as she thought it was not her place to say. This means Alfred could fall into his own trap. I think he hopes to create a picture of you running to the door with the pearls' box half open and dropping the curls of hair. He's going to be as sick as a parrot when she says she found them in his bedroom!"

"Well, what happens if he does not ask her where?"

"Then you have the delicious pleasure of cross-examining the witness and asking her yourself."

"Well, stone me! I might just win the hand of the fair maiden yet!" said Julian, realising all was not lost.

"Oh, you've no worries about Amanda; she would happily walk on coals if she thought it would save you. You have but to ask 'The *fair maiden'* for her hand in marriage and she's all yours."

"Steady on, old boy; one minute I am facing 5 years in jail for carrying out a one-man crime wave and the next it's down to the theft of some pearls which, as you know, I did not take and now you say I can have the girl and the pearls and… crumbs, the whole estate!"

"What do you mean the whole estate? I think Mr Alfred owns that!"

"Oh no, he doesn't. It is merely held by him in trust for Amanda until she is 21 and then once she gets married, she gets the house and land."

"How on earth do you know that?"

"Because on the back of a copy of this mortgage deed I was supposed to have stolen, which the judge has all but thrown out, was a copy of Amanda's dad's Will. I don't think Alfred realised it was pinned to the back of the copy he tossed to me, but it explains why every boyfriend she has had gets the elbow.

"Well, wait till Adrian hears this; he's all but admitted you're the guy for Amanda."

Chapter 13

Mum's the word!

Back at Cooper's Bank, you may have thought nothing out of the ordinary was going on. Alfred was back in his study poring over his law books and mentally rehearsing the cross-examination of his two remaining witnesses, nothing unusual there. Then he was invariably encamped in his study and, once again, took his evening meal with books piled about him.

Amanda was trying not to think too much about Julian. After all, over these recent weeks, she had hardly had any communication from him.

Adrian, however, was plotting a rather special event which he kept very much to himself just in case it all went wrong at the last moment.

Amanda did find it slightly unusual for him to suggest they go to Evensong the previous Sunday, but she had agreed, in some way feeling a little spiritual guidance from above could not go amiss.

The hymns were all ones that both Amanda and Adrian enjoyed singing and they found themselves in competition with the choir who were rather short in number that evening. At the end of the service, Amanda stayed in her pew for a few moments of quiet reflection and even a secret prayer. This gave Adrian the opportunity to go over and speak to the vicar, the Reverend Stanley Stanshawe, who had christened both Amanda and Adrian.

As it happened, Sunday afternoon and evening was the only time Harman had off and he often went to the Evensong service. He was sitting at the back and was in earshot of what Adrian was saying to the vicar. What he thought he heard rather surprised him, but then he thought it would be rather wonderful. It was something about the banns being read and a date of Saturday 7th September. 'Why, that is in just under a weeks' time. Better get some extra supplies in,' he thought, 'but Alfred will not agree to some extra expenditure'. And while Amanda could agree to it, he got the impression that Miss Amanda may be the last to know.

Harman was indeed right as he found out the Thursday evening when Adrian came and saw him. "We thought we would arrange a special party for Julian on Saturday," he said.

"Is that wise? Mr Radiant could be behind bars by then."

"Well, that's true but two of those called for jury service are people I know and who met Julian. I'm fairly sure they will see this as a witch hunt and find him not guilty."

"Well, I hope you are right, Mr Adrian, but should they be on the jury if they were here or known to Julian?"

"They could have been kicked off at the start, but it seems Alfred, if he recognised them, thought he would be able to make such a forceful case that it would not matter, and Julian was hardly going to object. I'll mention it to Amanda that we are having just a very small get-together so you can get the expenditure agreed, but one of the things we are going to need is a tier cake like you have at wedding breakfasts."

"Well, you scoundrel, Mr Adrian! Perhaps you did not see me at the back of church last Sunday, but do I assume there could be a Mrs Radiant in charge shortly?"

"Spot on, Harman, but for heaven's sake, keep it under your hat. If Alfred gets wind of this, he'll be having the vicar arrested on some pretext to stop the wedding. Oh, and at this stage, Amanda does not know of the impending nuptials either, and for that matter neither does Julian, although it is obvious from things they have both said recently that it's very much what they hope for. Harry has been keeping me up to date with a number of things the trial has revealed. Did you know that Amanda inherits this house and land if she gets married?"

"I thought Mr Alfred owned it all!"

"No, we have never actually seen the Will, but apparently, it is held in trust. Once she is over 21 and married, it's all hers."

"Does that not concern you, your elder sister taking it all?"

"No, that's fine by me. After all, I have plans to work abroad at least for a few years, so, if Amanda is looking after Cooper's Bank, that's fine by me."

Well, I had better start thinking how I am going to get all this prepared. I shall need a bit of help on the day if not before."

"Well, Mary would have been able to help but she will be in court tomorrow. She is our special witness; a sort of secret weapon."

"I hope it's legal," said Harman.

"Absolutely," said Adrian. "All she is going to do is tell the truth, **the whole truth** and nothing but the truth, except it is not the truth that Alfred is quite expecting! Now I'll leave you to it, I must ensure Amanda has not got anything else planned for Saturday".

Adrian went off to find Amanda. She was not downstairs, so he went upstairs to her bedroom.

"Mandy, there you are..." Adrian entered the bedroom and, as if by some premonition, lying across the bed was her mother's wedding dress.

"Well, does it fit you?"

"Yes, it does actually."

"So, are you getting married, Mandy?"

"Yes," she said.

"Who to - anybody I know?"

"Julian, of course!" The words had hardly left her lips when she burst into tears.

"Mandy, Mandy, it's okay. You can marry him. I won't mind; in fact,

I shall be very pleased to have him as a brother-in-law."

"But Alfred will have him in irons by tomorrow and where would we live?"

"That's where you are wrong. Two things have happened since yesterday and both solve your problems."

"What do you mean?"

"Well, shall we just say things are not going to go all Alfred's way? Shall we say where there's a *Will* there's a way. Now, are you happy to have a small gathering here on Saturday to celebrate Julian's acquittal? Only Harman will need a bit of extra dosh to prepare a suitable feast for the un-condemned man."

"Well, yes, but are you sure?"

"Don't worry, Mandy. I have everything under control."

Adrian gave his sister a big hug and then left the room. 'Now, what next? Bridesmaid, Julia, I think. I'll ring her and find out what she is up to this evening. I wonder if she's got a suitable dress? The boys can all nip off to Moss Bros but with girls, their needs are bit more complicated,' he thought.

Downstairs, Adrian rang the Walkers. "Can I speak to Julia?"

"Who's calling?"

"Adrian Charlecote." A few moments later, a voice said,

"Julia here."

"Hi, it's Adrian. What are you up to this evening?"

"Nothing much; may pop down to the pub to see some of the lads."

"Great! Can I come and pick you up, say 7:30? There is something very important I need to speak to you about... alone!"

"Well, okay, but what's this all about?"

"Sorry, can't say over the phone; mum's the word; see you at 7:30 sharp."

At a few minutes to seven, Adrian borrowed Amanda's car on some pretext that he needed to see Harry and sped off to Whites, the

Walkers' home.

Adrian timed it so he arrived exactly on time and, helpfully, Julia emerged from the front door allowing Adrian to stay in the car as he hoped not to be seen.

Once they set off, Julia raised the matter of this secret straight away.

"Well," said Adrian, "as you may have gathered, Amanda is smitten with Julian and does not know if she should elope to a foreign land with him or go off to a nunnery."

"Adrian, what are you on about? What are you up to? Not one of your elaborate jokes, I hope."

"No, no, but seriously, how about being a bridesmaid on Saturday?"

"A bridesmaid on Saturday, this Saturday... whose bridesmaid... what are you planning?"

"A wedding, of course, Amanda and Julian's."

"But Julian could be serving at Her Majesty's pleasure by then! Anyway, they would need a licence and there isn't time for the banns to be read."

They've been read; I have the certificate. You know the day of the party, Julian turned up just after breakfast and he and Amanda went riding. Well, when they got to the church, they were just standing there and in came this priest who gets them to go through the marriage service and enters their names and addresses and so forth into the banns book."

"But how do you know this?"

"Julian told me; and what's more, Jane told me she was in church about three weeks ago and the vicar read out the Banns for the third time of asking. Jane rang me and I said not to worry, it was a bit of a joke that had probably gone too far, but that it did not matter; after all, you don't have to get married because the banns have been read. However, in this case, it does help, if you see what I mean. So, I am arranging Julian and Amanda's wedding for Saturday at 12 noon sharp. I've agreed the time with the vicar. It was quite difficult to stop him going over to Amanda and discussing it with her, but I said everything was explained by this other vicar, Merver I think his name was. Fortunately, he got cornered by the lady who does the flowers, so we managed to escape before Amanda discovered what I was up to, but I need a bridesmaid and you seem the obvious choice. After all, you've known her for years even went to the same school and all that, so how about it? Have you got a dress you can wear? It does not need to be white; just special."

"Well, since you ask, yes, I have just got my dress for Charlotte's bash. You don't know her - she's a work colleague - I could wear that."

"Stupendissimo! Now, mum's the word, you understand. You can tell everybody to be at the church on Saturday but don't tell them why until shortly before they arrive, or at least Saturday morning at the earliest; after all, it could all go horribly wrong, but by Friday evening, we will know the result of Julian's trial and then I will have to get him to propose."

"No pressure then. Adrian, you're a bit of a romantic on the side, aren't you? Well, this could be some weekend if everything pans out. Perhaps I shouldn't say this, but my father has been acting very strangely recently and it's just possible that Julian's my half-brother - something to do with the war. A Mr Ragiant came to see my father and although I could not quite hear what was going on, it was something to do with Julian. Also, I overheard him talking to Inspector Rathbone and it was the phrase he used - *"upsetting for my whole family"* - and it seemed to me he included Julian in the word family.

"Mr Ragiant! Oh crumbs, he would want to be at the wedding and I don't know how to contact him; *and* he has to come all way the way from France."

"Oh, we may be in luck there. Amanda told me she had written to him to tell him the date of the trial so he may turn up at court tomorrow."

"Well, let's hope so."

"Right, we are here, and I need a stiff drink and you, Adrian, are definitely buying."

After about an hour at the Red Lion and having met a few of the crew who were primed to be available on Saturday but weren't told what they were meant to be available for, Adrian and Julia left, and, having taken her back to Whites, he returned to Cooper's Bank to find Mr Ragiant in residence.

'Great,' thought Adrian, 'one less problem to overcome', but to ensure he did not disappear immediately after the trial, he got Amanda to insist that he stay on for a few days.

Chapter 14

"That can't be right."

Everybody at Cooper's Bank was a little edgy when they rose on Friday morning. They all seemed to sense this was make or break as if history would be written today, although probably only Adrian knew the full reason for this apparent cosmic event that was affecting everybody's state of mind.

In no time at all it was 10:00 am and all the parties were in court. Judge Wentworth entered the court and all rose.

The judge looked towards Mr Charlecote; "Mr Charlecote, before we proceed further, do you intend to keep this theft of deeds on the charge sheet?"

"No, Your Honour, having considered the matter carefully, I believe there is insufficient evidence to continue with that part of the charge."

"Thank you, Mr Charlecote. We will therefore continue with your prosecution on the single charge of stealing a double string of pearls, but I have to say at this stage I do wonder if you are not making a mischief out of the law. However, on the basis we will have some more compelling evidence before us, you may continue. Call your next witness, please."

"I call Mr Julian Radiant."

A hush fell over the court room. Even Julian was slightly confused and Harry, peering down from the gallery, looked puzzled. Alfred, however, seemed like a man on a mission as indeed he was; if he lost this case, he would be a laughingstock. He therefore started carefully to ensure he could get Julian to trip up and admit to the theft.

Julian, having initially been a bit worried, thought, 'I still have my own trap to spring'. He thought back to the day before the party where he had been £2M in the red and by keeping his nerve, had changed his loss position into a £1.6M gain. 'Revenge is a dish best served cold', he thought.

"Mr Radiant," said Mr Charlecote, "much weight has been given to the fact that you could not have had time to steal the pearls and put them in your car and also go back to steal a brooch and then come down the front stairs. However, it occurs to me that you had hours to steal the pearls. You could have stolen them earlier in the evening and then just gone up to steal a small brooch, simply to pander to Miss Amanda's rather silly game."

Julian pondered on this for a moment and then said,

"Well, we had the food, then we were outside playing bat and trap for about an hour and a bit; then I suppose I was free, but I get the feeling that it must have been about 10:30 pm before Amanda left the note. After all, I noticed there was the slight smell of prawns coming from the note, and there were some prawns available on the buffet and vaguely remember her eating some."

"Quite the forensic investigator," said Alfred sarcastically. "That still leaves an hour and a half; plenty of time for you to go up and down staircases."

"Well, as I said to the Inspector, once, or rather if, I had taken the pearls, why not jump in my car and drive off there and then?"

"Because you are a very cunning man, Mr Radiant. You thought the theft of the pearls would not be noticed until the early hours and perhaps not even until the next day. You did not expect Amanda to go back and check shortly before the time for your assignation. Admit it, Mr Radiant; you planned it all. Up to Amanda's bedroom about, say, 10:45 pm, grab the pearls, place them in your car, then back to mingle a bit then at about twenty to twelve, you revisit the bedroom to get the required trinket to satisfy the task."

"I had to read the note to know where to go and that was inside the case, and it was locked."

"Mr Radiant, all these minor points still don't take up hours. You find the key, you open the case, you read the note, toss it to one side, skedaddle with the pearls and place them in your car. Then, as I say, nip back again just before the witching hour. Why don't you just admit it, Mr Radiant? You are guilty; you know you are guilty, and you are wasting this court's time by continuing with your pretence that some mysterious other being took the pearls. Stop being in denial, Mr Radiant; just admit it and we can all go home. I cannot believe the jury can think anything other than it is you who is the agile man who has been pilfering jewellery from half the houses in Buckinghamshire; now, Mr Radiant, just tell the judge the truth."

Julian said nothing but sat there looking a bit sad. He slumped a little as if realising he had been found out and even the judge was thinking it must be him. There was no point in his continuing with his pleading of innocence.

After a couple of minutes of Julian just looking mournful, the judge asked, "Do you have any further questions for the accused?"

"No, Your Honour," said Alfred.

"Very well; you can step down, Mr Radiant."

Julian was play-acting to perfection; he even half stumbled as he took the seat reserved for the defence.

"Do you have any further witnesses you wish to call, Mr Charlecote?"

"No, Your Honour. I think the jury have heard enough to make the appropriate decision."

The judge turned to Julian, and, more out of politeness than procedure, asked, "Do you wish to call any witnesses in your defence, Mr Radiant?"

"Yes, Your Honour. I call Miss Mary Downing."

Alfred's head turned and looked at Julian, convinced that he was only going to trap himself further if he brought up the finding of the curls of hair.

Mary was sworn in and sat down in the witness box. She was expecting to be cross-examined by the slightly scary Mr Alfred, so smiled when Julian approached her.

"Miss Downing, can you tell the court what your job is, please."

"I clean for the Charlecotes at Cooper's Bank and sometimes I help out Mr Harman, the butler, if there is going to be a do on, especially at weekends."

"Now, please answer my question very carefully and precisely, Miss Downing.

Did you find anything on Tuesday 10th July, that is the Tuesday immediately following the party?"

"Yes."

"Can you tell the court what you found?"

"Two curls of hair tied with small ribbons."

By now, with at least two of the audience in the gallery knowing what Julian was up to, a noticeable tension was building across the court, and even Harry was thinking this Julian would make a better barrister than he. Alfred, however, was not concerned; they merely proved that the case containing the pearls had been opened in the bedroom, lending weight to the fact that he had been there.

The judge, on the other hand, was slightly intrigued. Why was Julian questioning a witness who had been on the prosecution's list and why the dramatics? He did not want this trial to become a game of charades or some magic trick, but at the same time, he could not fault Julian. Indeed, he was thinking that Mr Alfred Charlecote had met his match here and Mr Radiant would only be found guilty by the good offices of the jury rather than by Mr Charlecote's conduct of the case.

Julian had deliberately paused at this point and pretended to be examining some papers as if he was struggling to find some keynote to ask Mary about.

"Miss Downing, I want you to think very carefully before you answer the next question. Can you please tell us precisely where you found these curls of hair?"

Mary could compose herself no longer and a big smile crept across her face while Harry and Adrian were leaning forward in the gallery on tenterhooks.

"In Mr Alfred Charlecote's bedroom, on the floor by the dressing table."

"Yes!" said both Harry and Adrian under their breath. Meanwhile, Amanda and then most of the gallery started whispering, "I don't believe it" and "I told you he was innocent."

Alfred rushed over to Mary, and, without waiting for the judge to allow him to cross-examine the witness, said loudly, "Surely you are mistaken; you mean Amanda's bedroom!"

"No, it was your bedroom. I always do your bedroom on Tuesdays."

"Are you sure it wasn't Friday, and you are getting muddled with the days and which room you were in?"

"No. You can ask Miss Amanda - she knows when I gave her the hair curls; it was Tuesday."

"But that can't be right."

At this point, the judge intervened.

"This witness is under oath, and you will not badger her, Mr Charlecote. Furthermore, I see her reasoning very clearly. I am not allowing this charade to continue any longer. I am bringing this trial to a close."

Then, addressing the jury, he said, "I had misgivings about proceeding with this trial from the start. I believe in this instance, while you are here to deliberate on the theft of some pearls, the evidence is so weak and doubtful that I must direct you to find the defendant not guilty."

A small cheer went up from the Gallery.

"I must have quiet, or I will have the gallery cleared. Do you wish to retire to consider your verdict?

The foreman of the jury turned about, and it was clear they were all nodding not guilty and thus turned back to the judge.

"No, Your Honour,

We find the defendant, Julian Radiant, not guilty."

The words had hardly left the foreman's lips before another cheer went up.

The judge looked up at the gallery and realised it was hopeless asking them to be quiet, so, waiting for a lull, he said, "Mr Radiant, you are free to go." And with that, the court erupted again with cheers and clapping. Judge Wentworth, with a slight smile on his face, rose and left the court.

Chapter 15

A family reunion.

Outside the court, there was much cheering as Julian emerged. He was all smiles but was anxiously looking around for Amanda who did not seem to be among the crowd. Adrian came up to him and said, "I think a drink is in order and this time you really have earned it, old boy," and he marched Julian across the road to the Golden Fleece.

"Now," said Adrian, whispering in his ear, "I have a little task for you. You need to propose to my sister!"

"What?" exclaimed Julian. "I mean, will she have me? Why, I have only had one full day with her and..."

"Julian, old chap, if you don't marry her, not only will she not be liveable with, but she is in danger of losing her birth right. She inherits Cooper's Bank as soon as she marries, but the point is she loves you and that's a fact, so don't let me down now. After all, everything is arranged."

"Well, should I not be asking Alfred if he is her guardian?"

"No way, man; she's over 21. After all, this guardian bit is a tad overdone. It's just Alfred's way of ensuring he does not lose the house. After all, you know the score; you discovered it yourself."

"Well, I can't say I had not thought about it. After all, I've had weeks of thinking about it, but always thought it would never happen with this court case taking over my life."

By now, the two of them had reached the pub and, on entering, went to the rear where Harry had been under instruction to escort Amanda and Gabriel Ragiant straight away, ahead of the crowd.

On spying Amanda, Julian froze on the spot, as if he was about to cross into an alternative universe.

Adrian, however, soon unfroze the hesitant Julian by shouting, "Get this man a drink, someone, before he dies of thirst!"

A peal of laughter spread across the room and Julian, now with flagon in hand, stood before Amanda saying rather politely, "Your good health, Miss, and to you, Grandpa".

They both smiled and then cries of 'speech!' came from the throng about him. By now, Julian was warming to the occasion, and, as if he was back in court, started slowly but with a theatrical air.

"My lords, ladies and gentlemen, and all you country folk," (there was a brief peal of laughter at this remark then he continued), "I must first thank my honourable adviser Harry for his work and diligent research which allowed me the *'Coup de grace'* that saved me from a spell of correction at Her Majesty's pleasure. I would also like to thank you, Adrian, especially for always being so friendly to me, an outsider. And, to the lovely lady here present before me," (at this he looked Amanda straight in the eyes, and, kneeling down before her said) "will you marry me?"

There was a sudden silence as everybody looked to Amanda who practically fell off the stool she was sitting on. Then, trying to comprehend what had just happened, she said, "Eh, yes… I mean, oh, yes, yes, **yes**!"

With this, the whole pub was in uproar, and even people unconnected with the group came across, and then, realising what had taken place, began clapping.

"Well," said Julian, "I think the drinks are on me…" and then he paused as he realised, "but I haven't any money, well, only two quid."

At this point, with tears in his eyes, his grandfather stepped forward. "I buy the drinks. Oh, I am so happy; she is such a lovely girl, and you make sure you look after her."

"Oh, don't worry, Grandpa; I will," and with his arm now around Amanda, he gave her a long passionate kiss, leaving the rest of the crowd to hoot and clap.

Adrian then came up, forcing his way between them, and, placing one arm across Amanda's shoulder and one across Julian's, he said, "Right, chaps, it's all arranged for tomorrow 12 noon at St Mary's Church; don't be late."

"What?!" they both said. "Tomorrow?!"

"Well, you've had the rehearsal and the banns have been read, Harman's all geared up for the wedding breakfast and Julia is all set to be your bridesmaid. I just need to take this chap down to Moss Bros and it's all fixed."

"Well, better do what the man says, darling. We chaps need to look the part, but I never thought I'd be married by lunchtime."

"That's what you said last time!" exclaimed Amanda. With that, they both burst out laughing.

Julian then went over to his grandfather. "Now I die happy." he said. "She is so like your mother."

"Mon grand-père, I need you at my wedding. You will be there, won't you? Where are you staying?

"Of course, I be there. I am staying with Amanda."

"Great, then you can escort her to the wedding and give her away; to me, that is," and he laughed.

That afternoon, there was much frantic preparation going on. At Cooper's Bank, Harman, now with a big smile on his face, was excelling himself with his usual faultless attention to detail. Then, along with Mary, who had now returned from her triumph at court that morning, was busy preparing a buffet to feed at least as many as had been at the party back in July. He had also ordered flowers and bouquets for both bride and bridesmaid. The cake with three tiers had been delivered that morning even before the verdict was known and thus quickly hidden in the pantry.

Alfred had vanished from the scene which was just as well. He had hurried off to his chambers at Lincolns Inn Fields in London, realising that he had better get prepared for any briefs that had come his way before the news of his defeat at the hands of a mere stockbroker got around.

In Aylesbury, the gang, that is Adrian, Julian and a few more of Adrian's friends who had been roped in to be ushers, entered Moss Bros to be fitted out.

Amanda returned with Julia to Cooper's Bank where Amanda tried on her mother's wedding dress. A few stitches were needed to ensure a perfect fit and even Julia thought she looked stunning and was now becoming almost jealous. She then put on her bridesmaid's dress; she'd had the foresight to bring it with her to court. They stood before a large mirror on the landing. "Don't we look the bees' knees?" said Julia and they both collapsed in a fit of giggles.

Downstairs, Mr Ragiant was quietly taking a nap in a large armchair in the Conservatory; after all, he'd had a rather busy and emotional day. However, on waking, he thought he should, at least out of courtesy, see if a reconciliation could not be made with Julian's father, and, plucking up his courage, asked if Harman knew the number of Mr Walker. "I am sure it will be in the phone book or on the list under the phone." So, having found and dialled the number, Harman handed him the phone and left him alone.

Saturday morning arrived all too early for some -Julian at the hotel in town; the Charlecotes at Cooper's Bank; the Walkers at Whites and even the Reverend Stanley Stanshawe climbed out of his bed saying a prayer for pleasant day. Only he looked out of the window to be greeted by a damp rainy morning. Mrs Stanshawe, however, was perhaps more upbeat and faithful than the rest. "Don't worry," she said. "Rain before seven, fine before eleven."

"I hope so," replied the vicar.

Unbeknown even to Adrian, the lads that looked after the horses at the stables next door had decided they were not going to be left out and had been up half the night and just as the hall clock chimed for the quarter hour at 11:15 that morning, they turned up at the front door with two horses bedecked with white plumes and drawing a small trap also suitably decorated.

Adrian was more pleased than anyone as the one thing he had forgotten was how Amanda was meant to get to the church, and he was busy trying to clean a rather dirty car when the carriage appeared.

Thus, at 11:20, Adrian sped off into town to collect Julian and drive to the church in a still-dirty car, while the bride, the bridesmaid and her sponsor, Mr Ragiant, followed a few minutes later in the trap.

With the church already packed, the clock struck twelve. The organ piped up and Amanda, on the arm of Mr Ragiant, walked slowly up the aisle arriving at the chancel step in front of the vicar and beside Julian, with Adrian acting as best man on his right. Julia, as bridesmaid, was behind, keeping an eye on the frail Gabriel Ragiant who was determined to deliver his charge to Julian's side.

The vicar then went through the first part of the service and, having asked them to confess *any impediment why they should not be joined in holy matrimony*, as well as asking the assembled congregation the same, he paused for a moment. It was at this point that even the vicar was slightly stunned by the complete silence that had spread across the church. All knew of a reason yesterday morning, but today, no such reason existed, and a visible and collective sigh of relief was felt when the vicar continued to ask Julian and then Amanda if they consented to be joined in holy matrimony.

"Who giveth this woman to be married to this man?"

"I do, with all my blessings" said Gabriel, who, having performed this sacred duty, quietly receded to sit on the pew behind him.

The service then proceeded without a hitch. Then, as the choir sang an anthem, the party proceeded into the vestry to sign the register and receive their marriage certificate. The surprise to all was that Mr Victor Walker strode purposefully up the aisle and into the vestry, and, placing his hand on Julian's shoulder, said to a rather dumfounded audience, "I think, son, I had better act as a witness and at least start to put right what has been wrong with my family until now". Julian turned, and, slightly confused and a little embarrassed, said softly, "So, I was right, you are my father and that means Julia, we are brother and sister?"

"Yes," answered Julia. "I had worked that out some days ago, although I could not be certain until now."

"Well done, Dad! Thank you; now we really can celebrate. It is not every day you gain a daughter and a son!"

Le fin

Lightning Source UK Ltd.
Milton Keynes UK
UKHW022040231222
414397UK00009B/403

9 781802 278903